PRAISE FOR
FINDING AUDREY

"*Finding Audrey* stands on its own."
—Time.com

"Sweet and hilarious." —*Justine* magazine

★ "An outstanding tragicomedy that gently
explores mental illness, the lasting effects
of bullying, and the power of friends and
loving family to help in the healing."
—*Kirkus Reviews*, Starred

"Kinsella's knack for humor and sensitivity
shine." —*Publishers Weekly*

"With her trademark wit and sass, Kinsella
sensitively broaches the complexities of
young adult mental health." —*Booklist*

"A beautiful balance of angst, humor, and
family drama." —*VOYA*

"An adorable, heartwarming story. . . .
Kinsella is spot-on in her descriptions of
anxiety, providing an honest look at the
disorder through Audrey's therapies and
recovery." —*BookPage*

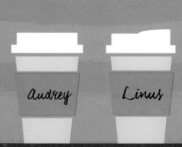

Audrey   Linus

THE NEW YORK TIMES BESTSELLER

FINDING AUDREY

BY SOPHIE KINSELLA

THE SHOPAHOLIC SERIES

Shopaholic to the Stars

Confessions of a Shopaholic

Shopaholic Takes Manhattan

Shopaholic Ties the Knot

Shopaholic & Sister

Shopaholic & Baby

Mini Shopaholic

◆ ◆ ◆

OTHER NOVELS

I've Got Your Number

Can You Keep a Secret?

The Undomestic Goddess

Remember Me?

Twenties Girl

Wedding Night

FINDING AUDREY

SOPHIE KINSELLA

Doubleday Canada

Paperback edition published by Doubleday Canada, 2016

Doubleday Canada and colophon are registered trademarks of Penguin Random
House of Canada Limited

Library and Archives Canada Cataloguing in Publication

Kinsella, Sophie, author
Finding Audrey / Sophie Kinsella.

ISBN 978-0-385-68501-6 (paperback)

I. Title.

PZ7.K626Fi 2016   j823'.92   C2014-907504-9

Printed and bound in the USA

Published in Canada by Doubleday Canada,
a division of Penguin Random House Canada Limited

www.penguinrandomhouse.ca

10 9 8 7 6 5 4 3

Penguin
Random House
DOUBLEDAY CANADA

To all my children,
who in their different ways
have helped inspire this book

OMG, Mum's gone insane.

Not normal Mum-insane. Serious insane.

Normal Mum-insane: Mum says, "Let's all do this great gluten-free diet I read about in the *Daily Mail*!" Mum buys three loaves of gluten-free bread. It's so disgusting our mouths curl up. The family goes on strike and Mum hides her sandwich in the flower bed and next week we're not gluten free anymore.

That's normal Mum-insane. But this is serious insane.

She's standing at her bedroom window, which overlooks Rosewood Close, where we live. No, *standing* sounds too normal. Mum does not look normal. She's teetering, leaning over the edge, a wild look in her eye. And she's holding my brother Frank's computer. It's balanced precariously on the window ledge. Any minute, it'll crash down to the ground. That's seven hundred pounds' worth of computer.

Does she realize this? Seven hundred pounds. She's always telling us *we* don't know the value of money. She's always saying stuff like "Do you have any idea how hard it is to earn ten pounds?" and "You wouldn't waste that electricity if you had to pay for it."

Well, how about earning seven hundred pounds and then deliberately smashing it on the ground?

Below us, on the front lawn, Frank is scampering about in his *Big Bang Theory* T-shirt, clutching his head and gibbering with panic.

"Mum." His voice has gone all high-pitched with terror. "Mum, that's my *computer*!"

"I know it's your computer!" Mum cries hysterically. "Don't you think I know that?"

"Mum, please, can we talk about this?"

"I've tried talking!" Mum lashes back. "I've tried cajoling, arguing, pleading, reasoning, bribing . . . I've tried everything! EVERYTHING, Frank!"

"But I need my computer!"

"You do not need your computer!" Mum yells, so furiously that I flinch.

"Mummy is going to *throw the computer*!" says Felix, running onto the grass and looking up in disbelieving joy. Felix is our little brother. He's four. He greets most life events with disbelieving joy. A lorry in the street! Ketchup! An extra-long chip! Mum throwing a computer out of the window is just another one on the list of daily miracles.

"Yes, and then the computer will break," says Frank fiercely. "And you won't be able to play *Star Wars* ever again, ever."

Felix's face crumples in dismay and Mum flinches with fresh anger.

"Frank!" she yells. "Do not upset your brother!"

Now our neighbours across the close, the McDuggans, have come out to watch. Their twelve-year-old son, Ollie, actually yells, "Noooo!" when he sees what Mum's about to do.

"Mrs. Turner!" He hurries across the street to our lawn and gazes up pleadingly, along with Frank.

Ollie sometimes plays *Land of Conquerors* online with Frank if Frank's in a kind mood and doesn't have anyone else to play with. Now Ollie looks even more freaked out than Frank.

"Please don't break the computer, Mrs. Turner," he says, trembling. "It has all Frank's backed-up game commentaries on it. They're so funny." He turns to Frank. "They're really funny."

"Thanks," mutters Frank.

"Your mum's really like . . ." He blinks nervously. "She's like Goddess Warrior Enhanced Level Seven."

"I'm what?" demands Mum.

"It's a *compliment*," snaps Frank, rolling his eyes. "Which you'd know if you played. Level Eight," he corrects Ollie."

"Right," Ollie hastily agrees. "Eight."

"You can't even communicate in English!" Mum flips. "Real life is not a series of levels!"

"Mum, please," Frank chimes in. "I'll do anything. I'll stack the dishwasher. I'll phone Grandma every night. I'll . . ." He casts wildly about. "I'll read to deaf people."

Read to deaf people? Can he actually hear what he's saying?

"Deaf people?" Mum explodes. "Deaf people? I don't

3

need you to read to deaf people! You're the bloody deaf one around here! You never hear anything I say! You always have those wretched earphones in—"

"Anne!"

I turn to see Dad joining the fray, and a couple of neighbours are stepping out of their front doors. This is officially a Neighbourhood Incident.

"Anne!" Dad calls again.

"Let me do this, Chris," says Mum warningly, and I can see Dad gulp. My dad is tall and handsome in a car advert way, and he *looks* like the boss, but inside, he isn't really an alpha male.

No, that sounds bad. He's alpha in a lot of ways, I suppose. Only Mum is *even more alpha*. She's strong and bossy and pretty and bossy.

I said bossy twice, didn't I?

Well. Draw your own conclusions from that.

"I know you're angry, sweetheart," Dad's saying soothingly. "But isn't this a little extreme?"

"Extreme? He's extreme! He's addicted, Chris!"

"I'm not addicted!" Frank yells.

"I'm just saying—"

"What?" Mum finally turns her head to look at Dad properly. "What are you saying?"

"If you drop it there, you'll damage the car." Dad winces. "Maybe shift to the left a little?"

"I don't care about the car! This is tough love!" She tilts the computer more precariously on the window ledge and we all gasp, including the watching neighbours.

"*Love?*" Frank is shouting up at Mum. "If you loved me you wouldn't break my computer!"

4

"Well, if you loved me, Frank, you wouldn't get up at two a.m. behind my back to play online with people in Korea!"

"You got up at two a.m.?" says Ollie to Frank, wide-eyed.

"Practicing." Frank shrugs. "I was *practicing*," he repeats to Mum with emphasis. "I have a tournament coming up! You've always said I should have a goal in life! Well, I have!"

"Playing *Land of Conquerors* is not a goal! Oh God, oh God . . ." She bangs her head on the computer. "Where did I go wrong?"

"Oh, Audrey," says Ollie suddenly, spotting me. "Hi, how are you?"

I shrink back from my position at my bedroom window in fright. My window is tucked away on a corner, and no-one was meant to notice me. Least of all Ollie, who I'm pretty sure has a tiny crush on me, even though he's two years younger than me and barely reaches up to my chest.

"Look, it's the celebrity!" quips Ollie's dad, Rob. He's been calling me "the celebrity" for the last four weeks, even though Mum and Dad have separately been over to ask him to stop. He thinks it's funny and that my parents have no sense of humour. (I've often noticed that people equate "having a sense of humour" with "being an insensitive moron.")

This time, though, I don't think Mum or Dad has even heard Rob's oh-so-witty joke. Mum is still moaning "Where did I go wroooong?" and Dad is peering at her anxiously.

"You didn't go wrong!" he calls up. "Nothing's wrong! Darling, come down and have a drink. Put the computer down . . . for now," he adds hastily at her expression. "You can throw it out of the window later."

Mum doesn't move an inch. The computer is rocking still more precariously on the windowsill, and Dad flinches. "Sweetheart, I'm just thinking about the car . . . We've only just paid it off . . ." He moves towards the car and holds out his hands, as though to shield it from plummeting hardware.

"Get a blanket!" says Ollie, springing to life. "Save the computer! We need a blanket. We'll form a circle . . ."

Mum doesn't even seem to hear him.

"I breast-fed you!" she shrieks at Frank. "I read you *Winnie-the-Pooh*! All I wanted was a well-rounded son who would be interested in books and art and the outdoors and museums and maybe a competitive sport . . ."

"*LOC* is a competitive sport!" yells Frank. "You don't know anything about it! It's a serious thing! You know, the prize pot in the international *LOC* competition in Toronto this year is six million dollars!"

"So you keep telling us!" Mum erupts. "So, what, you're going to win that, are you? Make your fortune?"

"Maybe." He gives her a dark look. "If I get enough *practice.*"

"Frank, get real!" Her voice echoes around the close, shrill and almost scary. "You're *not* entering the international *LOC* competition, you're *not* going to win the bloody six-million-dollar prize pot, and you're *not* going to make your living from gaming! IT'S NOT GOING TO HAPPEN!"

A MONTH EARLIER

It all begins with the *Daily Mail*. Quite a lot of things in our house begin with the *Daily Mail*.

Mum starts twitching in that way she does. We've had supper and cleared away and she's been reading the paper with a glass of wine—"Me time," she calls it—and she's paused at an article. I can see the headline over her shoulder:

THE EIGHT SIGNS YOUR CHILD IS ADDICTED TO COMPUTER GAMES

"Oh my God," I hear her murmur. "Oh my *God*." Her finger is moving down the list and she's breathing fast. As I squint over, I catch a subheading:

7. IRRITABILITY AND MOODINESS.

Ha. Ha ha.

That's my hollow laugh, in case you didn't get that.

I mean, seriously, *moodiness*? Like, James Dean was a

moody teenager in *Rebel Without a Cause* (I have the poster, best film poster ever, best movie ever, sexiest movie star ever, why, why, why did he have to die?). So James Dean must therefore have been addicted to video games? Oh, wait.

Exactly.

But there's no point saying any of this to my mum, because it's logical and my mum doesn't believe in logic, she believes in horoscopes and green tea. Oh, and of course the *Daily Mail*.

THE EIGHT SIGNS MY MUM IS ADDICTED TO THE *DAILY MAIL*:

1. She reads it every day.

2. She believes everything it says.

3. If you try to take it out of her grasp, she pulls it back sharply and says "Leave it!" like you're trying to kidnap her precious young.

4. When it runs a scare story about Vitamin D, she makes us all take our shirts off and "sunbathe." (Freeze-bathe, more like.)

5. When it runs a scare story about melanoma, she makes us all put on sunscreen.

6. When it runs a story about "the face cream that really DOES work," she orders it that moment. Like, she gets out her iPad then and there.

7. If she can't get it on holiday, she gets major withdrawal symptoms. I mean, talk about irritability and moodiness.

8. She once tried to give it up for Lent.

She lasted half a morning.

Anyway. There's nothing I can do about my mum's tragic dependency except hope that she doesn't do *too* much damage to her life. (She's already done major damage to our living room, after reading an "Interiors" piece about "Why not hand paint all your furniture?")

So then Frank ambles into the kitchen, wearing his black I MOD, THEREFORE I AM T-shirt, his earphones in and his phone in his hand. Mum lowers the *Daily Mail* and stares at him as though the scales have fallen from her eyes.

(I've never understood that. Scales?

Anyway. Whatever.)

"Frank," she says, "how many hours have you played on your computer games this week?"

"Define computer games," Frank says, without looking up from his phone.

"What?" Mum looks at me uncertainly, and I shrug. "You know. Computer games. How many hours? FRANK!" she yells, as he makes no move to respond. "How many hours? Take those things out of your ears!"

"What?" says Frank, taking his earphones out. He blinks at her as though he didn't hear the question. "Is this important?"

"Yes this is important!" Mum spits. "I want you to tell me how many hours you're spending per week playing computer games. Right now. Add it up."

"I can't," says Frank calmly.

"You can't? What do you mean, you *can't*?"

"I don't know what you're referring to," says Frank, with elaborate patience. "Do you mean literally computer games? Or do you mean all screen games, including Xbox and PlayStation? Do you include games on my phone? Define your terms."

Frank is such a moron. Couldn't he *see* Mum was in one of her pre-rant build-ups?

"I mean anything that warps your mind!" says Mum, brandishing the *Daily Mail*. "Do you realize the dangers of these games? Do you realize your brain isn't developing properly? Your BRAIN, Frank! Your most precious organ."

Frank gives a dirty snigger, which I can't help giggling at. Frank is actually pretty funny.

"I'll ignore that," says Mum stonily. "It only goes to prove what I was saying."

"No it doesn't," says Frank, and opens the fridge. He takes out a carton of chocolate milk and drains it, straight from the carton, which is gross.

"Don't do that!" I say furiously.

"There's another carton. Relax."

"I'm putting a limit on your playing, young man." Mum bats the *Daily Mail* for emphasis. "I've just about had enough of this."

Young man. That means she's going to drag Dad into it. Any time she starts using *young man* or *young woman*, sure enough the next day there's some ghastly family meeting, where Dad tries to back up everything Mum says, even though he can't follow half of it.

Anyway, not my problem.

◆ ◆ ◆

Until Mum arrives in my bedroom that evening and demands,

"Audrey, what *is Land of Conquerors*?"

I look up from *Grazia* and survey her. She looks tense. Her cheeks are pink and her right hand is all clenched, as if it's just come off a computer mouse. She's been Googling "computer game addiction," I just *know* she has.

"A game."

"I know it's a game!" Mum sounds exasperated. "But why does Frank play it all the time? *You* don't play it all the time, do you?"

"No." I've played *LOC*, and I really don't get the obsession. I mean, it's OK for an hour or two.

"So what's the appeal?"

"Well, you know." I think for a moment. "It's exciting. You get rewards. And the heroes are pretty good. Like, the graphics are amazing, and they just released this new warrior team with new capabilities, so . . ." I shrug.

Mum looks more bewildered than ever. The trouble is, she doesn't play games. So it's kind of impossible to convey to her the difference between *LOC 3* and, say, *Pac-Man* from 1985.

"They show it on YouTube," I say in sudden inspiration. "People do commentaries. Hang on."

As I'm finding a clip on my iPad, Mum sits down and looks around the room. She's trying to act casual, but I can sense her beady blue eyes scanning my piles of stuff, looking for . . . what? Anything. Everything. The truth is, Mum and I haven't done casual for a while. Everything is loaded.

With everything that's happened, that's one of the saddest things of all. We can't be normal with each other anymore.

The tiniest thing I say, Mum's all over it, even if she doesn't realize it. Her brain goes into overdrive. *What does it mean? Is Audrey all right? What's Audrey really saying?*

I can see her looking closely at a pair of old ripped jeans on my chair, as though they hold some dark significance. Whereas in fact the only significance they hold is: I've grown out of them. I've shot up about three inches in the last year, which makes me five eight. Quite tall for fourteen. People say I look like Mum, but I'm not as pretty as her. Her eyes are *so* blue. Like blue diamonds. Mine are wishy-washy—not that they're particularly visible right now.

Just so you can visualize me, I'm fairly skinny, fairly nondescript, wearing a black vest-top and skinny jeans. And I wear dark glasses all the time, even in the house. It's ... Well. A thing. My thing, I suppose. Hence the "celebrity" quips from Rob our neighbour. He saw me in my dark glasses, getting out of the car in the rain, and he was all like, "Why the shades? Are you Angelina Jolie?"

I'm not trying to be *cool*. There's a reason.

Which, of course, now you want to know.

I assume.

OK, it's actually quite private. I'm not sure I'm ready to tell you yet. You can think I'm weird if you like. Enough people do.

"Here we are." I find a clip of some *LOC* battle with "Archy" commentating. "Archy" is a YouTuber from Sweden who makes videos that Frank loves. They consist of "Archy" playing *LOC* and making funny commentaries on the game, and as I expected, it takes me forever to explain this concept to Mum.

"But why would you watch someone else playing?" she keeps saying, baffled. "Why? Isn't that a complete waste of time?"

"Well. Anyway." I shrug. "That's *LOC.*"

There's silence for a moment. Mum is peering at the screen like some professor trying to decipher an ancient Egyptian code. There's an almighty explosion and she winces.

"Why does it always have to be about *killing*? If I designed a game it would centre on ideas. Politics. Issues. Yes! I mean, why not?" I can tell her brain's firing up with a new idea. "What about a computer game called *Discuss*? You could keep the competitive element, but score points by debating!"

"And *that* is why we're not squillionaires," I say, as though to a third party.

I'm about to find another clip, when Felix comes running into the room.

"Candy Crush!" he says in delight as soon as he spies my iPad, and Mum gasps in horror.

"How does he know about that?" she demands. "Turn it off. I'm not having another addict in the family!"

Oops. It may possibly have been me who introduced Felix to *Candy Crush*. Not that he has any idea how to play it properly.

I close down the iPad and Felix stares at it, crestfallen. *"Candy Crush!"* he wails. "I want to play *Candy Cruuuuush*!"

"It's broken, Felix." I pretend to press the iPad. "See? Broken."

"Broken," affirms Mum.

Felix looks from us to the iPad. You can sense his mind is working as hard as his four-year-old brain cells will let him.

"We must buy a plug," he suggests, with sudden animation, and grabs the iPad. "We can buy a plug and fix it."

"The plug shop's closed," says Mum, without missing a beat. "What a shame. We'll do it tomorrow. But guess what? We're going to have toast and Nutella now!"

"Toast and Nutella!" Felix's face bursts into joyous beams. As he throws up his arms, Mum grabs the iPad from him and gives it to me. Five seconds later I've hidden it behind a cushion on the bed.

"Where did the *Candy Crush* go?" Felix suddenly notices its disappearance and screws up his face to howl.

"We're taking it to the plug shop, remember?" says Mum at once.

"Plug shop." I nod. "But hey, you're going to have toast and Nutella! How many pieces are you going to have?"

Poor old Felix. He lets Mum lead him out of the room, still looking confused. Totally outmaneuvered. That's what happens when you're four. Bet Mum wishes she could pull that trick on Frank.

So now Mum knows what *LOC* is. And knowledge is power, according to Kofi Annan. Although, as Leonardo da Vinci said: "Where there is shouting, there is no true knowledge," which might apply better to our family. (Please don't think I'm super-well-read or anything. Mum bought me a book of quotations last month and I flick through it when I'm watching telly.)

Anyway, "knowledge is power" isn't really happening here, because Mum has no power over Frank at all. It's Saturday evening, and he's been playing *LOC* ever since lunchtime. He disappeared into the playroom straight after pudding. Then there was a ring at the doorbell and I scuttled out of the way into the den, which is my own private place.

Now it's nearly six and I've crept into the kitchen for some Oreos, to find Mum striding around, all twitchy. She's exhaling and looking at the clock and exhaling again.

"They're all computer addicts!" she says in a sudden burst. "I've asked them to turn off about twenty-five times! Why can't they do it? It's a simple switch! On, off."

"Maybe they're on a level—" I begin.

"Levels!" Mum cuts me off savagely. "I'm tired of hearing about levels! I'm giving them one more minute. That's it."

I take out an Oreo and prise it open. "So, who's with Frank?"

"A friend from school. I haven't met him before. Linus, I think he's called . . ."

Linus. I remember Linus. He was in that school play, *To Kill a Mockingbird,* and he played Atticus Finch. Frank was Crowd.

Frank goes to Cardinal Nicholls School, which is just up the road from my school, Stokeland Girls' School, and sometimes the two schools join together for plays and concerts and stuff. Although to be truthful, Stokeland isn't "my school" anymore. I haven't been to school since February, because some stuff happened there. Not great stuff.

Whatever.

Anyway. Moving on. After that, I got ill. Now I'm going to change schools and go down a year so I won't fall behind. The new school is called the Heath Academy and they said it would be sensible to start in September, rather than the summer term when it's mainly exams. So, till then, I'm at home.

I mean, I don't do *nothing.* They've sent me lots of reading suggestions and maths books and French vocab lists. Everyone's agreed it's vital I keep up with my schoolwork and "It will make you feel so much better, Audrey!" (It so doesn't.) So sometimes I send in a history essay or something and they send it back with some red comments. It's all a bit random.

Anyway. The point is, Linus was in the play and he was a really good Atticus Finch. He was noble and heroic and everyone believed him. Like, he has to shoot a rabid dog in one scene and the prop gun didn't work on our night, but no-one in the audience laughed or even murmured. That's how good he was.

He came round to our house once, before a rehearsal. Just for about five minutes, but I still remember it.

Actually, that's kind of irrelevant.

I'm about to remind Mum that Linus played Atticus Finch, when I realize she's left the kitchen. A moment later I hear her voice:

"You've played enough, young man!"

Young man.

I dart over to the door and look through the crack. As Frank strides into the hall after Mum, his face is quivering with fury.

"We hadn't reached the end of the *level*! You can't just switch off the game! Do you understand what you did, just then, Mum? Do you even know how *Land of Conquerors* works?"

He sounds properly irate. He's stopped right underneath where I am, his black hair falling over his pale forehead, his skinny arms flailing, and his big, bony hands gesticulating furiously. I hope Frank grows into his hands and feet one day. They can't stay so comically huge, can they? The rest

17

of him has to catch up, surely? He's fifteen, so he could still grow a foot. Dad's six foot, but he always says Frank will end up taller than him.

"It's fine," says a voice I recognize. It's Linus, but I can't see him through the crack. "I'll go home. Thanks for having me."

"Don't go home!" exclaims Mum, in her best charming-to-visitors voice. "Please don't go home, Linus. That's not what I meant at all."

"But if we can't play games ..." Linus sounds flummoxed.

"Are you saying the only form of socialising you boys understand is playing computer games? Do you know how sad that is?"

"Well, what do you suggest we do?" says Frank sulkily.

"I think you should play badminton. It's a nice summer's evening, the garden's beautiful, and look what I found!" She holds out the ropy old badminton set to Frank. The net is all twisted and I can see that some animal has nibbled at one of the shuttlecocks.

I want to laugh at Frank's expression.

"Mum ..." He appears almost speechless with horror. "Where did you even *find* that?"

"Or croquet!" adds Mum brightly. "That's a fun game."

Frank doesn't even answer. He looks so stricken by the idea of croquet, I actually feel quite sorry for him.

"Or hide-and-seek?"

I give a snort of laughter and clap my hand over my mouth. I can't help it. Hide-and-seek.

"Or Rummikub!" says Mum, sounding desperate. "You always used to love Rummikub."

"I like Rummikub," volunteers Linus, and I feel a tweak of approval. He could have legitimately laid into Frank at this point; walked straight out of the house and put on Facebook that Frank's house sucks. But he sounds like he wants to please Mum. He sounds like one of those people who look around and think, well, why *not* make life easier for everyone? (I'm getting this from three words, you understand.)

"You want to play Rummikub?" Frank sounds incredulous.

"Why not?" says Linus easily, and a moment later the two of them head off towards the playroom. (Mum and Dad repainted it and called it the Teenage Study when I turned thirteen, but it's still the playroom.)

Next moment, Mum is back in the kitchen, pouring herself a glass of wine.

"There!" she says. "They just need a little guidance. A little parental control. I simply opened their minds. They're not *addicted* to computers. They just need to be reminded what else is out there."

She's not talking to me. She's talking to the Imaginary *Daily Mail* Judge, who constantly watches her life and gives it marks out of ten.

"I don't think Rummikub is a very good game for two," I say. "I mean, it would take ages to get rid of all your tiles."

I can see Mum's thoughts snagging on this. I'm sure she has the same image I do: Frank and Linus sitting grimly across from each other at the Rummikub table, hating it and deciding that all board games are rubbish and total pants.

"You're right," she says at last. "Maybe I'll go and play with them. Make it more fun."

She doesn't ask me if I want to play too, for which I'm grateful.

"Well, have a good time," I say, and take out the Oreo packet. I scoot through the kitchen into the den, and it's only as I'm zapping on the telly that I hear Mum's voice resounding through the house from the playroom.

"I DIDN'T MEAN ONLINE RUMMIKUB!"

Our house is like a weather system. It ebbs and flows, flares up and subsides. It has times of radiant blue bliss, days of grey dismalness and thunderstorms that flare up out of nowhere. Right now the storm's coming my way. Thunder-lightning-thunder-lightning, Frank-Mum-Frank-Mum.

"What *difference* does it make?"

"It makes every difference! I told you not to go on those computers anymore!"

"Mum, it's the same bloody game!"

"It's not! I want you off that screen! I want you playing a game with your friend! IN REAL LIFE!"

"It's no fun with two players. We might as well play, I don't know, bloody Snap."

"I know!" Mum is almost shrieking. "That's why I was coming to play with you!"

"Well, I didn't bloody KNOW THAT, DID I?"

"Stop swearing! If you swear at me, young man . . ."

Young man.

I hear Frank make his Angry Frank noise. It's a kind of rhinoceros bellow slash scream of frustration.

"*Bloody* is not swearing," he says, breathing hard, as though to rein in his impatience.

"It is!"

"It's in the Harry Potter films, OK? *Harry Potter.* How can it be swearing?"

"What?" Mum sounds wrong-footed.

"Harry Potter. I rest my case."

"Don't you walk away from me, young man!"

Young man. That makes three. Poor Dad. He will so get an earful when he arrives home—

"Hi." Linus's voice takes me by surprise, and I jump round in shock. Like, I literally jump. I have pretty sharpened reflexes. *Oversensitive.* Like the rest of me.

He's at the doorway. *Atticus Finch* shoots through my brain. A lanky, brown-haired teenager with wide cheekbones and floppy hair and one of those smiles like an orange segment. Not that his teeth are orange. But his mouth makes that segment shape when he smiles. Which he's doing now. None of Frank's other friends ever smile.

He comes into the den and instinctively my fists clench in fear. He must have wandered off while Mum and Frank were fighting. But no-one comes in this room. This is my space. Didn't Frank tell him?

Didn't Frank *say*?

My chest is starting to rise in panic. Tears have already started to my eyes. My throat feels frozen. I need to escape. I need— I can't—

No-one comes in here. *No-one is allowed to come in here.*

I can hear Dr. Sarah's voice in my head. Random snippets from our sessions.

Breathe in for four counts, out for seven.

Your body believes the threat is real, Audrey. But the threat isn't real.

"Hi," he tries again. "I'm Linus. You're Audrey, right?"

The threat isn't real. I try to press the words into my mind, but they're drowned out by the panic. It's engulfing. It's like a nuclear cloud.

"Do you always wear those?" He nods at my dark glasses.

My chest is pumping with terror. Somehow I manage to edge past him.

"Sorry," I gasp, and tear through the kitchen like a hunted fox. Up the stairs. Into my bedroom. Into the furthest corner. Crouched down behind the curtain. My breath is coming like a piston engine and tears are coursing down my face. I need a Clonazepam, but right now I can't even leave the curtain to get it. I'm clinging to the fabric like it's the only thing that will save me.

"Audrey?" Mum's at the bedroom door, her voice high with alarm. "Sweetheart? What happened?"

"It's just . . . you know." I swallow. "That boy came in and I wasn't expecting it . . ."

"It's fine," soothes Mum, coming over and stroking my head. "It's OK. It's totally understandable. Do you want to take a . . ."

Mum never says the words of medication out loud.

"Yes."

"I'll get it."

She heads out to the bathroom and I hear the sound of water running. And all I feel is stupid. Stupid.

◆ ◆ ◆

So now you know.

Well, I suppose you don't know—you're guessing. To put you out of your misery, here's the full diagnosis: Social

22

Anxiety Disorder, General Anxiety Disorder, and Depressive Episodes.

Episodes. Like depression is a sitcom with a fun punch line each time. Or a TV box set loaded with cliffhangers. The only cliffhanger in my life is "Will I ever get rid of this shit?" and believe me, it gets pretty monotonous.

At my next session with Dr. Sarah I tell her about Linus and the whole anxiety attack thing, and she listens thoughtfully. Dr. Sarah does everything thoughtfully. She listens thoughtfully, she writes thoughtfully with beautiful loopy writing, and she even taps at her computer thoughtfully.

Her surname is McVeigh but we call her Dr. Sarah because they brainstormed about it in a big meeting and decided first names were approachable but *Dr.* gave authority and reassurance, so Dr. First Name was the perfect moniker for the children's unit.

(When she said "moniker" I thought they were all going to be renamed Monica. Seriously, for about ten minutes, till she explained.)

The children's unit is at a big private hospital called St. John's, which Mum and Dad got the insurance for through Dad's job. (The first question they ask when you arrive is not

"How do you feel?" It's "Do you have insurance?") I lived here for six weeks, after Mum and Dad worked out that there was something really wrong with me. The trouble is, depression doesn't come with handy symptoms like spots and a temperature, so you don't realize at first. You keep saying "I'm fine" to people when you're not fine. You think you *should* be fine. You keep saying to yourself: "Why aren't I fine?"

Anyway. At last Mum and Dad took me to see our GP and I got referred and I came here. I was in a bit of a state. I don't really remember those first few days very well, to be honest. Now I visit twice a week. I could come more often if I wanted—they keep telling me that. I could make cupcakes. But I've made them, like, fifty-five zillion times and it's always the same recipe.

After I've finished telling Dr. Sarah about the whole hiding-behind-the-curtain thing, she looks for a while at the tick box questionnaire I filled in when I arrived. All the usual questions.

Do you feel like a failure? Very much.

Do you ever wish you didn't exist? Very much.

Dr. Sarah calls this sheet my "symptoms." Sometimes I think, *Shall I just lie and say everything's rosy?* But the weird thing is, I don't. I can't do that to Dr. Sarah. We're in this together.

"And how do you feel about what happened?" she says in that kind, unruffled voice she has.

"I feel stuck."

The word *stuck* comes out before I've even thought it. I didn't know I felt stuck.

"Stuck?"

"I've been ill *forever.*"

"Not forever," she says in calm tones. "I first met you . . ." She consults her computer screen. "March sixth. You'd probably been ill for a while before that without realizing. But the good news is, you've come such a long way, Audrey. You're improving every day."

"Improving?" I break off, trying to speak calmly. "I'm supposed to be starting a new school in September. I can't even talk to people. One new person comes to the house and I freak out. How can I go to school? How can I do anything? What if I'm like this forever?"

A tear is running down my cheek. Where the *hell* did that come from? Dr. Sarah hands me a tissue without comment and I scrub at my eyes, lifting up my dark glasses briefly to do so.

"First of all, you will not be like this forever," says Dr. Sarah. "Your condition is fully treatable. *Fully treatable.*"

She's said this to me about a thousand times.

"You've made marked progress since treatment began," she continues. "It's still only May. I have every confidence you will be ready for school in September. But it will require—"

"I know." I hunch my arms round my body. "Persistence, practice, and patience."

"Have you taken off your dark glasses this week?" asks Dr. Sarah.

"Not much."

By which I mean *not at all.* She knows this.

"Have you made eye contact with anybody?"

I don't answer. I was supposed to be trying. With a family member. Just a few seconds every day.

I didn't even tell Mum. She would have made it into this huge palaver.

"Audrey?

"No," I mutter, my head down.

Eye contact is a big deal. It's the biggest deal. Just the thought makes me feel sick, right down to my core.

I know in my rational head that eyes are not frightening. They're tiny little harmless blobs of jelly. They're, like, a minuscule fraction of our whole body area. We all have them. So why should they bother me? But I've had a lot of time to think about this, and if you ask me, most people underestimate eyes. For a start, they're powerful. They have range. You focus on someone a hundred feet away, through a whole bunch of people, and they *know* you're looking at them. What other bit of human anatomy can do that? It's practically being psychic, is what it is.

But they're like vortexes too. They're infinite. You look someone straight in the eye and your whole soul can be sucked out in a nanosecond. That's what it feels like. Other people's eyes are limitless and that's what scares me.

There's quiet in the room for a while. Dr. Sarah doesn't say anything. She's thinking. I like it when Dr. Sarah thinks. If I could curl up in anyone's brain, I think it would be hers.

"I've had an idea for you." She looks up. "How do you feel about making a film?"

"What?" I look at her blankly. I was not expecting this. I was expecting a sheet with an exercise on it.

"A documentary film. All you need is a cheap little

digital video camera. Perhaps your parents will get you one, or we could find one here to lend you."

"And what will I do with it?"

I'm sounding deliberately stupid and uninterested because inside, I feel flustered. A film. No-one ever mentioned making a film before. Is that a thing? Is it the new version of cupcakes?

"I think this may be a good way for you to transition from where you are now to ..." Dr. Sarah pauses. "To where we want you to be. At first, you can film as the outsider. Fly-on-the-wall. Do you know what that means, 'fly-on-the-wall'?"

I nod, trying to hide my rising panic. This is happening too fast.

"Then, after a while, I'd like you to start interviewing people. Could you make eye contact with someone through a camera, do you think?"

I feel a blinding shaft of terror, which I tell myself to ignore, as my brain will often try to send me messages that are *untrue and I do not have to listen to them*. This is lesson one at St. John's: your brain is an idiot.

"I don't know." I swallow, feeling my fists clench up. "Maybe."

"Great." Dr. Sarah gives me her angelic smile. "I know this feels hard and scary, Audrey. But I think it will be a great project for you."

"OK, look, I don't understand ..." I pause, gaining control of myself; trying not to let tears of fright well up. I don't even know what I'm frightened of. A camera? A new idea? A demand on me which I wasn't expecting?

"What don't you understand?"

"What do I film?"

"Anything. Anything you come across. Just point the camera and shoot. Your house. The people in your house. Paint a portrait of your family."

"Right." I can't help snorting. "I'll call it *My Serene and Loving Family.*"

"If you like." She laughs. "I look forward to seeing it."

MY SERENE AND LOVING FAMILY—FILM TRANSCRIPT

INTERIOR. 5 ROSEWOOD CLOSE. DAY.

The camera pans around a cluttered family kitchen.

> **AUDREY (VOICE-OVER)**
> So, welcome to my documentary. This is
> the kitchen. This is the kitchen table.
> Frank hasn't cleared away his breakfast,
> he's revolting.

ANGLE ON: a scrubbed pine table, bearing a used cereal
bowl, a plate covered with crumbs, and a pot of
Nutella with a spoon sticking out.

> **AUDREY (V.O)**
> These are the kitchen cupboards.

ANGLE ON: a range of Shaker kitchen cupboards painted
grey. The camera pans slowly across.

> **AUDREY (V.O.)**
> This is stupid. I don't know what
> I'm supposed to be filming. This is
> the window.

ANGLE ON: a window to the garden, where we can see an
old swing set and a brand-new fire pit, still with
tags on. Camera zooms in on the fire pit.

> **AUDREY (V.O.)**
> That was my dad's birthday present. He
> should use it, really.

Camera swings shakily to door.

                    AUDREY (V.O.)
        OK, so I should introduce myself. I'm
        Audrey Turner and I'm filming this because—
                        (pause)
        Anyway. My mum and dad bought me this
        camera. They were all like, "Maybe
        you'll become a documentary maker!"
        I mean, they got super-excited and
        they spent far too much on this camera.
        I was like, just get me the cheapest
        thing, but they wanted to, so . . .

The camera moves jerkily through to the hall and
focuses on the stairs.

                    AUDREY (V.O.)
        That's the stairs. You can see that,
        right? You're not a moron.
                        (pause)
        I don't even know who you are. Who's
        watching this? Dr. Sarah, I suppose.
        Hi, Dr. Sarah.

The camera moves unsteadily up the stairs.

                    AUDREY (V.O.)
        So we're going upstairs now. Who lives
        in THIS house?

Camera focuses on a black lacy bra draped over the
bannisters.

                    AUDREY (V.O.)
        That's Mum's.
                        (beat)
        Actually, she may not want you to see that.

Camera turns a corner and focuses on an ajar door.

> **AUDREY (V.O.)**
> That's Frank's room, but I can't even
> go near it because of the stench. I'll
> zoom in.

Camera zooms in on an area of floor space covered
with trainers, dirty socks, a wet towel, three Scott
Pilgrim books, a half-empty bag of Haribo, all thrown
on top of each other.

> **AUDREY (V.O.)**
> The entire room's like that. Just so
> you know.

Camera moves away, along an upstairs landing.

> **AUDREY (V.O.)**
> And this is my mum and dad's room . . .

Camera focuses on a half-open door. From inside the
room, we hear a voice. This is MUM, Audrey's mum. She
is talking in a low, urgent voice which, nevertheless,
we can hear.

> **MUM (V.O)**
> I was talking about it at book
> group and Caroline said, "Does he
> have a girlfriend?" Well, he doesn't!
> Is THAT the problem? If he had a
> girlfriend, maybe he'd be out more,
> instead of hunched over that screen.
> I mean, why DOESN'T he have a
> girlfriend?

> **DAD (V.O.)**
> I don't know. Don't look at me like
> that! It's not my fault!

                    AUDREY (V.O.)
                   (sotto voce)
This is my mum and dad. I think they're
talking about Frank.

                     MUM (V.O.)
Well, I've had an idea. We need to
throw a party for him. Set him up with
some pretty girls.

                     DAD (V.O.)
A PARTY? Are you serious?

                     MUM (V.O.)
Why not? It would be fun. We used to
throw him some lovely parties.

                     DAD (V.O.)
When he was EIGHT. Anne, do you know
what teenage parties are like? What if
they knife each other and have sex on
the trampoline?

                     MUM (V.O.)
They won't! Will they?
Oh God . . .

The door closes slightly. The camera moves closer to
pick up the sound.

                     MUM (V.O.)
Chris, have you given Frank a father-
to-son talk?

                     DAD (V.O.)
No. Have you given him a mother-to-son
talk?

                    MUM (V.O.)
I bought him a book. It had pictures
of . . . you know.

                    DAD (V.O.)
            (sounds interested)
Did it? What kind of pictures?

                    MUM (V.O.)
You know.

                    DAD (V.O.)
I don't.

                    MUM (V.O.)
            (impatiently)
Yes you do. You can imagine.

                    DAD (V.O.)
I don't want to imagine. I want you to
describe them to me, very slowly, in a
French accent.

                    MUM (V.O.)
        (half giggling, half cross)
Chris, stop it!

                    DAD (V.O.)
Why should Frank have all the fun?

The door opens and DAD comes out. He is a handsome man
in his early forties, wearing a suit and holding a
scuba-diving mask. He jumps as he sees the camera.

                      DAD
Audrey! What are you doing here?

                    AUDREY (V.O.)
I'm filming. You know, for my project.

                            DAD

          Right. Right, of course.
                    (calls warningly)
          Sweetheart, Audrey's filming . . .

Mum appears at the door, dressed in a skirt and bra.
She claps her hands over her top half and shrieks when
she sees the camera.

                            DAD

          That's what I meant when I said
          "Audrey's filming."

                            MUM
                    (flustered)
          Oh, I see.

She grabs a dressing gown from the door hook and wraps
it around her top half.

                            MUM

          Well, bravo, darling. Here's to a
          great film. Maybe warn us next time
          you're filming?
          (glances at Dad and clears her throat)
          We were just discussing the . . . er . . .
          crisis in . . . the Middle East.

                            DAD
                    (nods)
          The Middle East.

Both parents look uncertainly at the camera.

OK, so the backstory. You'll want to know that, I suppose. *Previously, in Audrey Turner's life ...*

Except, Jeez. I can't go into it all again. Sorry, I just can't. I've sat in enough rooms with teachers, doctors, regurgitating the same story, using the same words, till it starts to feel like something that happened to someone else.

Everyone involved has started to feel unreal. All the girls at Stokeland Girls' School; Miss Amerson, our head teacher, who said I was deluded and seeking attention. (Attention. Irony God, are you listening?)

No-one ever quite found out why. I mean, we sort of found out why, but not *why.*

There was a big scandal, yadda yadda. Three girls were excluded, which is a record. My parents took me out of Stokeland instantly, and I've been at home ever since. Well, and hospital, which I told you about already. The idea is that

I "start again" at the Heath Academy. Only to "start again" you need to be able to "get out of the house," which is where I have a teeny problem.

It's not the outside *per se*. It's not trees or air or sky. It's the people. I mean, not all people. Probably not you; you'd be fine. I have my comfort people—people I can talk to and laugh with and feel relaxed with. It's just, they make up quite a small group. Tiny, you might call it, compared to, say, the world's population. Or even the number of people on an average bus.

I can eat supper with my family. I can go to see Dr. Sarah in my safe little bubble of car-waiting-room-Dr.-Sarah's-room-car-home. All the people in my therapy groups at St. John's—they're comfort people too. Because they're not a threat. (OK, OK, I *know* people aren't really a threat. But try telling my stupid brain that.)

It's everyone else who is the problem. People on the street, people at the front door, people on the phone. You have no idea how many people there are in the world until you start getting freaked out by them. Dr. Sarah says I may never be comfortable in massive crowds, and that's OK, but I have to "dial down" the thoughts that are telling me to panic. When she's telling me this, it seems totally reasonable, and I think "Yes! I can do that! Easy." But then a postman comes to the door and I run before I can even stop myself.

Thing is, I was never exactly *out there,* even when I was OK. In a bunch of girls, I was the one standing alone, hiding behind her hair. I was the one trying to join in chat about bras even though, hello, a bra? That would surely require a female shape. I was the one paranoid that everyone must be looking at me, thinking how uncool I was.

At the same time, I was the one who got shown off to all the visitors: "Our straight-A student, Audrey." "Our netball star, Audrey."

Top tip to all teachers reading this (i.e., none, probably): try *not* showing off the girl who cringes when anyone even looks at her. Because it's not that helpful. Also, it's not that helpful to say in the whole class's earshot: "She's the great hope of this year group, so talented."

Who wants to be the great hope? Who wants to be "so talented"? Who wants the entire rest of year to slide their eyes round like daggers?

I mean, I don't blame those teachers. I'm just saying.

So then. All the bad stuff happened. And I kind of slid off a cliff. And here I am. Stuck in my own stupid brain.

Dad says it's totally understandable and I've been through a trauma and now I'm like a small baby who panics as soon as it's handed to someone it doesn't know. I've seen those babies, and they go from happy and gurgling to howling in a heartbeat. Well, I don't howl. Not quite.

But I feel like howling.

You still want to know, don't you? You're still curious. I mean, I don't blame you.

Here's the thing: does it matter exactly what happened and why those girls were excluded? It's irrelevant. It happened. Done. Over. I'd rather not go into it.

We don't have to reveal everything to each other. That's another thing I've learned in therapy: it's OK to be private. It's OK to say no. It's OK to say, "I'm not going to share that." So, if you don't mind, let's just leave it there.

I mean, I appreciate your interest and concern, I really do. But you don't need to pollute your brain with that stuff. Go and, like, listen to a nice song instead.

INTERIOR. 5 ROSEWOOD CLOSE. DAY.

The camera pans around the hall and focuses on the hall tiles.

> **AUDREY (VOICE-OVER)**
> So, these are old Victorian tiles or whatever. My mum found them in a skip and made us lug them all home. It took FOREVER. We had a perfectly good floor, but she was all like, "These are history!" I mean, someone threw them out. Does she not realize that?

> **MUM**
> Frank!

Mum comes striding into the hall.

> **MUM**
> FRANK!
> (to Audrey) Where is your brother?
> Oh. You're filming.

She flicks back her hair and pulls in her stomach.

> **MUM**
> Well done, darling!

FRANK ambles into the hall.

> **MUM**
> Frank! I found these on Felix's playhouse.

She brandishes a bunch of sweet wrappers at him.

                        MUM

        First of all, I don't want you sitting on
        top of the playhouse, the roof is unstable
        and it's a bad example to Felix. Second of
        all, do you realize how toxic this
        sugar is to your body? Do you?

Frank doesn't reply, just glowers at her.

                        MUM

        How much exercise do you take per week?

                        FRANK

        Plenty.

                        MUM

        Well, it's not enough. We're going on
        a run tomorrow.

                        FRANK
                     (outraged)
        A run? Are you serious? A RUN?

                        MUM

        You need to get out more. When I was
        your age, I lived outside! I was always
        playing sport, enjoying nature, walking
        through the woods, appreciating the
        outside world . . .

                        FRANK

        Last week you said when you were our
        age you were "always reading books."

                        MUM

        Well, I was. I did both.

                    AUDREY
              (from behind camera)
          Last year you said when you were our
          age you were "always going to museums
          and cultural events."

Mum looks caught out.

                      MUM
                    (snaps)
          I was doing all of it. Anyway, we're
          going for a run tomorrow. This is non-
          negotiable.
                  (as Frank draws breath)
          Non-negotiable. NON-NEGOTIABLE, FRANK.

                     FRANK
          Fine. *Fine.*

                      MUM
                  (over-casually)
          Oh, and Frank. I was just wondering.
          There were some nice girls in your
          school play, weren't there? Anyone on
          the . . . you know? Horizon? You should
          ask them round!

Frank gives her a withering look. The doorbell rings
and Frank looks warningly at the camera.

                     FRANK
          Hey, Aud, this is Linus, if you want
          to . . . you know. Get out of the way.

                  AUDREY (V.O)
          Thanks.

                       42

Mum disappears into the kitchen. Frank heads towards the front door. The camera backs away but has a view of the front door.

Frank opens the front door to reveal LINUS.

> FRANK

Hey.

> LINUS

Hey.

Linus glances at the camera and it quickly swoops away and retreats.

Then, slowly, from a further distance, it comes back to rest on Linus's face. It zooms in.

I mean, I was just filming him because he's Frank's friend. It's just, you know. Family context or whatever.

OK. And he has a nice face.

Which I have watched on playback a few times.

The next day after breakfast Mum comes down in leggings, a pink crop top, and trainers. She has a heart rate monitor strapped round her chest and is holding a water bottle.

"Ready?" she calls up the stairs. "Frank! We're going! Frank! FRANK!"

After an age, Frank appears. He's wearing black jeans, a black T-shirt, his usual trainers, and a scowl.

"You can't run like that," says Mum at once.

"Yes I can."

"No you can't. Don't you have any athletic shorts?"

"*Athletic* shorts?"

Frank's look of disdain is so terrible, I give a snort.

"What's wrong with athletic shorts?" says Mum defensively. "That's the trouble with you young people. You're closed-minded. You're prejudiced."

You young people. Three words which signal that a Mumrant is coming. I look at her from the sitting room doorway and sure enough, the other signs are building. Her eyes are full of thoughts ... she clearly has things to say ... she's breathing fast ...

And bingo.

"You know, Frank, you only get one body!" She turns on him. "You have to treasure it! You have to take care of it! And what worries me is you seem to have no idea about health, no idea about fitness—all you want to eat is junk ..."

"We'll have robotic body-part replacements by the time we're your age," says Frank, unmoved. "So."

"Do you know how many people your age have diabetes?" Mum continues. "Do you know how many teens these days are obese? And don't even get me started on heart problems."

"OK, I won't get you started on heart problems," says Frank mildly, which seems to enrage her.

"And you know what it is? It's all the fault of these evil screens. Some children your age can't even get up off the couch!"

"How many?" retorts Frank.

"What?" Mum looks at him, puzzled.

"How many children my age can't even get up off the couch? Because that sounds like BS to me. Did you read it in the *Daily Mail*?"

Mum glares at him. "A significant number."

"Like, three. Because they broke their leg."

I can't help giggling, and Mum shoots me a glare too.

"You can mock me all you like," she says to Frank. "But I take my responsibility as a parent seriously. I will *not* let you become a couch potato. I will *not* let your arteries harden. I will *not* let you become a statistic. So come on. We're running. We'll start with a warm-up. Follow me."

She starts marching, pumping her arms at the same time. I recognize the moves from her Davina exercise DVD. After a moment Frank joins in, waving his arms around and rolling his eyes comically. I have to ball a fist into my mouth to stop laughing.

"Engage your core," Mum says to Frank. "You should do Pilates. Have you heard of an exercise called 'the plank'?"

"Give me a break," mutters Frank.

"Now, stretch . . ."

As they're bending over to stretch their hamstrings, Felix comes bouncing into the hall.

"Yoga!" he shouts in his joyous way. "I can do yoga. I can do yoga VERY FAST."

He lies on his back and kicks his legs in the air.

"Brilliant yoga," I tell him. "That's very fast yoga."

"And STRONG yoga." Felix looks at me seriously. "I am the strongest yoga."

"You are the strongest yoga," I agree.

"All right." Mum lifts her head. "So, Frank, we'll take it easy today, just a nice little run . . ."

"What about press-ups?" Frank interrupts. "Shouldn't we do some press-ups before we leave?"

"*Press-ups?*" Mum's face falls for an instant.

I've seen Mum doing press-ups along with Davina's DVD. It's not a pretty sight. She curses and sweats and gives up after about five. "Well . . . yes." She regains her composure. "Good idea, Frank. We could do a couple of press-ups."

47

"How about thirty?"

"Thirty?" Mum looks ashen.

"I'll start," says Frank, and drops to the floor. Before I know it, he's pumping his arms, lowering his face to the ground, and rising up rhythmically. He's really good. I mean, *really* good.

Mum is staring at him as though he's turned into an elephant.

"Aren't you going to join in?" says Frank, barely pausing.

"Right," says Mum, getting onto her hands and knees. She does a couple of press-ups, then stops.

"Can't you keep up?" says Frank, panting. "Twenty-three ... twenty-four ..."

Mum does a few more press-ups, then stops, puffing. She's really not enjoying this.

"Frank, *where* did you learn to do those?" she says as Frank finishes. She sounds almost cross, like he's fooled her.

"School," he says succinctly. "PE." He sits back on his knees and gives her a malicious little smile. "I can run too. I'm in the cross-country team."

"What?" Mum looks faint. "You didn't tell me."

"Shall we go?" Frank gets to his feet. "Only I don't want to turn into an obese teenage heart attack victim." As they head for the door, I hear him saying, "Did you know that most middle-aged women don't do enough press-ups? It was in the *Daily Mail.*"

◆　◆　◆

Forty minutes later they pant back into the hall. I say *pant.* Frank's barely broken a sweat, whereas Mum looks like she's going to collapse. Her face is red and her hair is dripping. She clutches onto the bannister for support, and breathes in and out like a traction engine.

"How was the running?" begins Dad, coming into the hall, and stops in alarm as he sees Mum. "Anne, are you OK?"

"I'm fine," manages Mum. "Fine. Frank did very well, in fact."

"Never mind Frank, what about you?" Dad is still staring at her. "Anne, did you overdo it? I thought you were fit!"

"I am fit!" she practically yells. "He tricked me!"

Frank is shaking his head sadly. "Mum's cardio could really do with some work," he says. "Mum, you only get one body. You need to *treasure* it."

And, winking at me, he ambles off to the playroom.

I mean, Frank has a point.

But Mum has a point too. Everyone has a point.

After he went for that run with Mum, Frank spent the next ten hours playing computer games. *Ten hours solid.* Mum and Dad were out all day with Felix, taking him to a series of birthday parties, and they told Frank to do his homework while they were out and Frank said yes and then he logged on and that was it.

Now it's Sunday morning and Mum is at tennis and Dad is doing something in the garden and I'm watching telly in the den when Frank appears at the door.

"Hey."

"Hey." My dark glasses are already on and I don't turn my head.

"Listen, Audrey, Linus is going to be spending a lot of time at our house. I think you should get to know him. He's on my *LOC* team."

I've already stiffened a little at the words *Linus* and *get to know him.*

"Why do I need to get to know him?" I counter.

"He feels weird coming to our house. Like, what happened the other day? When you ran away? It freaked him out a bit."

I scowl at Frank. I don't want to be reminded.

"He doesn't need to feel weird," I say, wrapping my arms round my knees.

"Well, he does. He thinks he upset you."

"Well, *tell* him. You know. About . . ."

"I have."

"Well then."

There's silence. Frank still doesn't look happy.

"If Linus doesn't want to come to our house, he might join another *LOC* team," he says. "And he's really good."

"Who else is on the team?" I swivel round to face Frank.

"These two guys from school. Nick and Rameen. They play online. But Linus and I are like the strategists. We're going to enter the *LOC* International Tournament, and the qualifiers are on July eighteenth, so we need a ton of practice. The prize pot is six million dollars."

"What?" I stare up at him.

"Seriously."

"You win six million dollars? Just for playing *LOC*?"

"Not 'just' for playing *LOC*," says Frank impatiently. "It's the new spectator sport." He looks more animated than I've seen him for ages. "They're holding it in Toronto and they're building like this massive stadium, and everyone's flying in. It's big money. This is what Mum and Dad don't get. These days, being a gamer is a career choice."

"Right," I say dubiously. I went to a careers fair at school.

I didn't see anyone sitting at a stall under a sign, BECOME A GAMER!

"So you need to make Linus feel comfortable here," Frank finishes. "I can't lose him off my team."

"Can't you go to his house?"

Frank shakes his head. "We tried. His granny's there. She's got some dementia thing. She won't leave us alone. She shouts and she cries and sometimes she doesn't know who Linus is, and she keeps taking everything out of the freezer. They, like, have to watch her all the time. Linus has to do all his homework at school."

"Right." I digest this. "Poor Linus. Well ... you know. Tell him it's all fine."

"He asked for your number, but ..." Frank shrugs.

"Right."

I don't have a phone number at the moment. Just to add to the party, I've become phone-averse. Not phobic, just averse.

Which Frank will never understand in a million years.

He heads off and I switch over to *You've Been Framed*. Felix comes in to watch it with me and we snuggle up on the sofa together. Felix is like a walking, talking teddy bear. He's soft and snuggly and if you press him in the tummy he laughs, every time. His head is a curly mass of blond like a dandelion clock and his face is constantly open and hopeful. You feel like nothing must ever go wrong for him, ever.

Which is, I guess, how Mum and Dad felt about me.

"So, how's school, Felix?" I say. "Are you still friends with Aidan?"

"Aidan has chicken pops," he tells me.

"Chicken pox?"

"Chicken pops," he corrects me, as though I'm an idiot. "Chicken *pops*."

"Oh, right." I nod. "I hope you don't get them."

"I will fight the chicken pops with my sword," he says importantly. "I'm a very strong fighter."

I take off my dark glasses and look into his round, open little face. Felix is the only one I can cope with looking at, eye to eye. My parents' eyes—forget it. They're full of worry and fear and too much knowledge. And kind of too much love, if that makes sense? If I look at them, it's like it all comes flooding back over me in a gush—mingled in with their anger, which is pretty righteous. I mean, it's not directed at me, obviously, but still. It feels toxic.

Frank's eyes are just a little freaked out every time he looks at me. It's like, *Help, my sister went nuts, what should I do?* He doesn't *want* to be freaked out, but he is. Well, of course he is. His sister hides inside and wears dark glasses— what else could he be?

But Felix's blue eyes are as transparent and clear and soothing as a drink of water. He knows pretty much nothing except the fact that he's Felix.

"Hello, you," I say, and press my face close against his.

"Hello, you." He squashes up even closer. "Do you want to build a snowman?"

Felix has a bit of a *Frozen* obsession, for which I don't blame him. I can relate to Queen Elsa myself. Only I'm not sure I'm going to melt the ice away by some random act of love. Chip it away with an ice pick, more like.

"Audrey." I hear Frank's voice. "Linus is here. He sent you this."

My dark glasses are back on as I raise my head from Felix. Frank is holding out a folded sheet of paper.

"Oh," I say, nonplussed, and take it from him. "OK."

As Frank heads away, I unfold the sheet and read the unfamiliar handwriting.

Hi. Sorry about the other day. I didn't mean to freak you out.
Linus

Oh God.

I mean, oh God on *so many levels*. First, he thinks he freaked me out. (Which he did, but not because he's freaky.) Second, he feels the need to apologise, which makes me feel bad. Third, what do I do now?

I think for an instant, then write underneath:

No, I'm sorry. I have this weird thing. It's not you.
Audrey

"Felix," I say. "Go and give this to Linus. *Linus*," I repeat as he stares at me with blank eyes. "Frank's friend. Linus? The big boy?"

Felix takes the paper and looks at it carefully for a moment. Then he folds it up, puts it in his pocket, and starts playing with a train.

"Felix, go on," I prod him. "Give it to Linus."

"But it fits in my pocket," he objects. "It's my pocket paper."

"It's not yours. It's a note."

"I want a *pocket paper*!" He screws up his face to howl.

For God's sake. In movies, they fix the note to a dog's collar and it trots off obediently, no nonsense.

"OK, Felix, you can have a pocket paper," I say in exasperation. "Whatever that is. Here you are." I rip a page out of a magazine, fold it up and stuff it in his pocket instead. "Now give this one to Linus. In the playroom."

When Felix finally leaves, I have no confidence that the note will reach its destination. It's a thousand times more likely that Felix will feed it into the waste disposal or the DVD player or just forget it exists. I turn up *You've Been Framed* and try to forget about it.

But about two minutes later there's Felix holding the note, saying excitedly, "Read it! Read the pocket paper!"

I unfold it—and Linus has added a new line. This is like a game of Consequences.

Frank explained. Must be tough for you.

I smooth the paper out on my knee and write:

It's fine. Well, you know, not fine. It is what it is. Hope you're winning. BTW, you were a great Atticus Finch.

I send the paper off with Felix the Wonder Dog and stare ahead at the screen—but I'm not watching *You've Been Framed* at all. I'm just waiting. I haven't done anything like this in forever. I haven't interacted with anyone except my safe people for . . . I don't know. Weeks. Months. Before I know it, Felix is back, and I grab the paper from him.

*Hey, thanks. Actually we're tanking. Frank
is shouting at me because I'm writing this.
You are a bad influence, Audrey.*

I look at the way he wrote my name. It feels intimate. It feels like he's taken hold of a piece of me. I try to hear his voice saying the word. *Audrey.*

"Draw the words," Felix is instructing me. He's totally got into his role as go-between. "Draw the words." He jabs the paper. "Words!"

I don't want to give this paper to Felix anymore. I want to fold it up and keep it somewhere where I can look at it in private. Study his writing. Think about him forming my name with his pen. *Audrey.*

I grab a fresh piece of paper from the side table where all my school supplies are stacked and scribble on it.

Well, it's been nice chatting or whatever. See you.

I send it off and half a minute later the reply comes:

See you.

I'm still holding the first paper; the one with my name on it. I press it to my face and inhale. I think I can smell his soap or shampoo or whatever.

Felix is pressing his nose to the other paper and he looks at me over the top with huge eyes.

"Your pocket paper smells like *poo*," he says, and bursts into laughter.

Trust a four-year-old to ruin the mood.

"Thanks, Felix." I ruffle his hair. "You're a great messenger."

"Draw more words," he says, patting the paper. "More words."

"We've finished our chat," I say, but Felix picks up a crayon and hands it to me.

"Make red words," he commands me. "Make 'Felix.' "

I write "Felix" and he gazes at it lovingly as I draw him close for another restoring cuddle.

I feel kind of exhilarated. And kind of emptied out. Which may seem like an overreaction, but then, in case you hadn't picked it up, I am the Queen of Overreaction.

The truth is, if you don't communicate with anyone new, ever, at all, then you lose the knack. And when you go back to it, it's sort of draining. Dr. Sarah has warned me about that. She says I should expect even the tiniest tasks or new steps to be a bit exhausting. And believe it or not, that silly little exchange of notes was.

Nice, though.

MY SERENE AND LOVING FAMILY—FILM TRANSCRIPT

INTERIOR. 5 ROSEWOOD CLOSE. DAY.

Camera pans towards a closed door.

> **AUDREY (VOICE-OVER)**
> So this is my dad's study.
> This is where he works when he's
> not at the office.

The door is pushed open by a hand. We see Dad, slumped at his desk, gently snoring. On the screen is an Alfa Romeo sports car.

> **AUDREY (V.O.)**
> Dad? Are you asleep?

Dad jumps up and hastily closes down his monitor.

> **DAD**
> I wasn't ASLEEP. I was thinking. So,
> have you wrapped your present for Mum?

> **AUDREY (V.O.)**
> That's why I'm here. Do you have any
> wrapping paper?

> **DAD**
> I do.

He reaches for a roll of wrapping paper and hands it to Audrey.

> **DAD**
> And look what else!

He produces a white pâtisserie box and opens it to reveal a large birthday cake. It is iced with a big "39."

There is silence for a moment.

> **AUDREY (V.O.)**
> Dad, why have you put "thirty-nine" on Mum's cake?

> **DAD**
> No-one's too old for a personalized birthday cake.
>> (He twinkles at the camera.)
> I know I'm not.

> **AUDREY (V.O.)**
> But she's not thirty-nine.

> **DAD**
>> (puzzled)
> Yes she is.

> **AUDREY (V.O.)**
> No she's not.

> **DAD**
> Yes she—

He breaks off and gasps. Aghast. He looks at the cake and back at the camera.

> **DAD**
> Oh God. Will she mind? No. Of course she won't mind. I mean, it's one year, what's the big deal—

> **AUDREY (V.O.)**
> Dad, she will SO mind.

Dad looks panic-stricken.

> **DAD**
> We need a new cake. How long do we have?

We hear the sound of a door bang downstairs.

> **MUM (OFF-SCREEN)**
> I'm home!

Dad looks freaked out.

> **DAD**
> Audrey, what shall I do?

> **AUDREY (V.O.)**
> We can fix it. We can change it to
> "thirty-eight."

> **DAD**
> With what?

He picks up a Tipp-Ex pot.

> **AUDREY (V.O.)**
> No!

There's a knocking at the door and Frank comes in.

> **FRANK**
> Mum's home. When are we doing her
> birthday tea?

Dad is uncapping a Sharpie.

> **DAD**
> I'll use this.

> **AUDREY (V.O.)**
> No! Frank, go to the kitchen. We
> need some writing icing or something.

Anything edible you can write with.
But don't let Mum know what you're doing.

                    FRANK
                  (baffled)
Anything edible you can write with?

                    DAD
Quick!

Frank disappears. The camera focuses on the cake.

                 AUDREY (V.O.)
How did you get her age wrong?
I mean, how did you manage that?

                    DAD
                (clutches head)
I don't know. I've spent all month
writing financial reports about next
year. My whole mind-set is next year. I
guess I lost a year somewhere.

Frank bursts into the room holding a squeezy bottle of
Heinz ketchup.

                 AUDREY (V.O.)
Ketchup? Seriously?

                    FRANK
                 (defensive)
Well, I didn't know!

Dad grabs the bottle.

                    DAD
Can we turn a "nine" into an "eight"
with ketchup?

                    FRANK
You won't fool her.

                 AUDREY (V.O.)
Go over the whole number with ketchup.
Make the whole thing a ketchup cake.

                    FRANK
Why would you ice a cake with ketchup?

                     DAD
              (hurriedly icing)
Mum loves ketchup. It's fine. It's all good.

OK, so here's a life lesson. Don't try fixing a birthday cake with ketchup. Tipp-Ex would have been better.

As Dad brought out the cake, Mum's jaw dropped. And not in a good way. I mean, if you take a white iced cake and pipe it all over with ketchup, it basically looks like the Texas Chainsaw Massacre. We all launched into "Happy Birthday" extra loudly, and as soon as we'd finished and Mum had blown out her (one) candle, Dad said, "Great! So let me take that away and cut it up—"

"Wait." Mum put a hand on his. "What IS that? That's not *ketchup*?"

"It's a Heston Blumenthal recipe," said Dad without blinking. "Experimental."

"Right." Mum still looked puzzled. "But isn't that . . ." Before anyone could stop her, she was scraping the ketchup off with a napkin. "I thought so! There's a message underneath."

"It's nothing," said Dad quickly.

"But it's piped in icing!" She wiped away the last blobs of ketchup and we all stared in silence at the smeared red-and-white cake.

"Chris," said Mum at last in an odd voice. "Why does it say thirty-nine?"

"It doesn't! It says thirty-eight. Look." Dad's hand traced over the vestiges of the ketchup. "That's an eight."

"Nine." Felix pointed confidently at the cake. "Number *nine.*"

"It's an eight, Felix!" said Dad sharply. "Eight!"

I could see Felix staring at the cake in puzzlement and felt a twinge of sympathy for him. How's he supposed to learn anything with nutso parents like ours?

"It's a nine, Felix," I whispered in his ear. "Daddy's joking."

"Do you think I'm thirty-nine?" Mum looked up at Dad. "Do I *look* thirty-nine? Is that what you think?" She squashed her face between her hands and glared at him. "Is this a thirty-nine-year-old face? Is that what you're telling me?"

I think Dad should have just junked the cake.

◆ ◆ ◆

So this evening my dad is taking my mum on a date for her birthday, which you can tell from the clouds of perfume that suddenly descend onto the landing. Mum isn't exactly subtle when she goes out. As she always tells us, her social life is practically nonexistent since having three kids, so when she goes out, she makes up for it with perfume, eye liner, hair spray and heels. As she totters down the stairs, I can see a little fake-tan blotch on the back of her arm, but I won't tell her. Not on her birthday.

"Will you be all right, darling?" She puts her hands on my shoulders and looks anxiously at me. "You've got our numbers. Any problems, you tell Frank to call, straightaway."

Mum knows I'm not brilliant with phones. Which is why Frank is officially on babysitting duty, not me.

"I'll be fine, Mum."

"Of course you will," she says, but doesn't let go of my shoulders. "Sweetheart, take it easy. Have an early night."

"I will," I promise.

"And, Frank." She looks up as he lopes into the hall. "You will be doing homework only. Because I am taking *this* with me."

She brandishes a power cable triumphantly, and Frank gapes.

"Did you—"

"Unplug your computer? Yes, young man, I did. I don't want that computer going on for a nanosecond. If you finish your homework you can watch TV or read a book. Read some Dickens!"

"Dickens," echoes Frank in disparaging tones.

"Yes, Dickens! Why not? When I was your age—"

"I know." Frank cuts her off. "You went to see Dickens live. And he rocked."

Mum rolls her eyes. "Very funny."

"So! Where's the birthday girl?" Dad comes hurrying down the stairs, bringing with him a cloud of aftershave. What is it with parents and too much perfume? "Now, are you guys OK?" He looks at me and Frank. "Because we'll only be round the corner."

My parents *cannot* leave the house. Mum has to do a final check on Felix, and Dad remembers he left the sprinkler on in the garden and then Mum wants to make sure that her Sky Plus is recording *EastEnders*.

Eventually we chivvy them out and look at each other.

"They'll be back in, like, an hour," predicts Frank, and heads off to the playroom. I follow him because I don't have much else to do, and I might read his new Scott Pilgrim. He goes to his computer station, rummages around in his school bag, and produces a power cable. Then he plugs in his computer and logs in, and up pops a game of *LOC*.

"Did you know Mum was going to take your cable?" I ask, impressed.

"She's done it before. I've got like five of them." His eyes glaze over as he starts playing and I know there's no point talking to him. I look around for the Scott Pilgrim, find it under an empty jumbo Hula Hoops packet, and curl up to read it on the sofa.

It seems about a moment later that I glance up to see Mum at the door, standing there in her heels. How did *that* happen?

"Mum." I blink, disoriented. "Aren't you out?"

"I came back for my phone." Her tone is sweet and ominous. "Frank? What are you doing?"

Oh God. Frank. Frank! My head whips round in apprehension. Frank is still moving his mouse around the mat, his earphones on.

"Frank!" Mum barks, and he looks up.

"Yes?"

"What are you doing?" says Mum, in the same sweet, ominous tone.

"Language lab," says Frank, without missing a beat.

"Language . . . what?" Mum seems wrong-footed.

"French homework. It's a vocab-testing program. I had to find an old power cable to do it. I thought you wouldn't mind."

He points at the monitor, and I see *armoire* floating round the screen in a big red font, followed by *wardrobe* in blue.

Wow. He must have moved quickly to get that up on-screen.

Actually, playing *LOC does* improve your reaction times. I mean, that's a real thing.

"You've been doing language lab all this time?" Mum glances at me with narrowed eyes, and I look away. I am not getting into this.

"I've been reading Scott Pilgrim," I say truthfully.

Mum's focus returns to Frank. "Frank, are you lying to me?"

"Lying?" Frank looks hurt.

"Don't give me that! Are you telling me, hand on heart, that you've been doing your homework and nothing else?"

Frank just stares at her for a moment. Then he shakes his head, his face sad.

"You adults. You think teenagers lie. You assume teenagers lie. That's the starting point. It's infinitely depressing."

"I don't assume anything—" begins Mum, but he cuts her off.

"You do! All of you make these easy, obvious, *lazy* assumptions that anyone under the age of eighteen is a pathological, dishonest, sub-human with no integrity. But we're people, just like you, and you don't seem to get that!" His face is suddenly passionate. "Mum, can't you just for once believe that your son might be doing the right thing? Can't you just for once give me an ounce of credit? But, look, if you want me to disconnect the computer and *not* do my French homework, that's fine. I'll tell the teacher tomorrow."

Mum looks thrown by Frank's little speech. In fact, she looks quite chastened.

"I didn't say you were lying! I just . . . Look, if you're doing French homework, that's fine. Carry on. I'll see you later."

She tip-taps down the hall, and a few moments later we hear the front door close.

"You're sick," I say, without looking up from my book. Frank doesn't reply. He's already engrossed in his game again. I turn a page and listen to Frank's mutterings, and wonder whether to go and make a hot chocolate, when suddenly there's the most almighty banging on the window, from outside.

"FRAAAAAAANK!!!"

I jump a mile, and feel myself start to hyperventilate. Mum is at the window, staring in, her face like some monstrous demon. I mean, I've never seen her look so furious. "Chris!" she's yelling now. "COME HERE! I'VE CAUGHT HIM RED-HANDED!"

How is she even up there? The windows of the playroom are like, eight feet off the ground outside.

I glance at Frank, and he looks genuinely a bit freaked out. He's closed down *LOC,* but she saw it. I mean, there's no way she didn't see it.

"You're for it," I say.

"*Shit.*" Frank scowls. "I can't believe she would *spy* on me."

"Chris!" Mum is yelling. "Help! I . . . *Arrrgh!*"

Her face disappears from the window and there's a loud *crunch.*

Oh my God. What just happened? I leap to my feet and run to the back door. The window of the playroom backs onto the garden, and as I head out, I can't see Mum anywhere. All I can see is Felix's playhouse, pulled up to the playroom window. But the roof seems to have broken, and—

No.

No way.

Mum's feet are poking out of it, still in her high heels.

Frank arrives on the back step, and sees what I'm looking at. He claps a hand over his mouth and I nudge him.

"Shut up! She might be hurt! Mum, are you OK?" I call, hurrying over to the playhouse.

"Anne!" Dad has arrived on the scene. "What happened? What were you doing?"

"I was looking in the window," comes Mum's stifled voice. "Get me *out* of here. I'm totally wedged in."

"I thought standing on the playhouse was a bad example to Felix, Mum," says Frank blandly, and I hear a furious gasp.

"You little . . ." It's probably a good thing Mum's voice is muffled at that point.

It takes me, Dad, and Frank together to haul Mum out of the playhouse, and I can't say it improves her mood. As she brushes her hair down, she's shaking with fury.

"Right, young man," she says to Frank, who is staring sullenly at the floor. "Well, you have cooked your goose. You are hereby banned from playing any computer games for . . . what do you think, Chris?"

"One day," says Dad firmly, just as Mum says, "Two months."

"Chris!" says Mum. "One *day*?"

"Well, I don't know!" says Dad defensively. "Don't put me on the spot."

Mum and Dad go off in a huddle and start whispering, while Frank and I wait awkwardly. I could go inside, I suppose, but I want to see how it all works out.

This is pretty lame, though, having to stand here while they whisper things like "Really get the message across" and "Make it count."

When I'm a parent I'm so going to work out the punishment *first*.

"OK." Dad eventually emerges from the huddle. "Ten days. No computer, no phone, nothing."

"Ten days?" Frank gives Dad one of his death-ray, please-die-now stares. "That is *so* out of proportion."

"It is not." Mum holds out her hand. "Phone, please."

"But what about my teammates? I can't just let them down. All that bullshit you give me about team spirit and 'all pull together'? And now I just let the side down?"

"What teammates?" Mum looks confused. "Is this the cross-country team?"

"My *LOC* teammates!" says Frank. "We're practicing for the tournament, like I've told you a billion times."

"A *computer game* tournament?" says Mum, in supreme disdain.

"The international *LOC* tournament! The prize pot is six million dollars! That's why Linus comes round the whole time! What do I say to him?"

"Tell him you're busy," says Mum crisply. "In fact, I'd rather Linus didn't come round anymore. I think you should find some friends with wider interests. And he upset Audrey."

"Linus is my friend!" Frank looks like he wants to explode. "You can't ban my frigging friends!"

OK, "frigging" was a mistake. I can see Mum drawing herself up like a cobra ready to strike.

"Please don't swear, Frank," she says icily. "And yes I can. This is my house. I control who comes in and out of it. You know Audrey had an attack when he was here?"

"She won't have any more attacks," says Frank at once. "Audrey's getting used to Linus, aren't you, Audrey?"

"He's OK," I say weakly.

"We'll discuss it," says Mum, giving Frank another icy stare. "For now, can I trust you to carry on with your homework tonight, and not produce another power cable, or do I have to cancel my birthday dinner, the one Dad and I have been looking forward to all month and which has already been half-ruined?" She looks at her legs. "My tights are *totally* ruined."

When she puts it like that, you do feel guilty. I mean, I feel bad, and I didn't even do anything, so I expect Frank feels worse. Although you never know, with Frank.

"Sorry," he mutters at last, and we watch silently as Mum and Dad head back round the house to the drive. We hear the car doors bang and they're off again.

"Ten days," says Frank at last, closing his eyes.

"It could have been two months," I say, trying to make him feel better, and immediately realizing this is a really lame and annoying thing to say. "I mean . . . sorry. That sucks."

"Yeah."

We go inside and I head towards the kitchen. I'm putting the kettle on for hot chocolate when I hear Frank at the door: "Listen, Audrey, you *have* to get used to Linus."

"Oh." I feel a weird little flip inside. It's that name. *Linus.* It does that to me.

"He needs to come round here. He needs a space to practice."

"But Mum won't let you play."

"Only for ten days." He waves his hand impatiently. "Then we need to get some serious hours in. It's the qualifiers coming up."

"Right." I spoon hot chocolate powder into my mug.

"So you can't freak out when you see him. I mean, not 'freak out,'" he amends at my expression. "Have an attack. Whatever. I know it's really serious. I know it's an illness, blah blah, I *know* all that."

Frank was dragged along to a family therapy group thing a couple of times. Actually, he was really sweet at it. He said some nice things to me. And about me, and what happened, and—

Anyway.

"The point is, Linus needs to come here, without Mum getting on my case," Frank is saying. "So you have to be able to look at him and not run away or whatever. OK?"

There's a pause. I pour boiling water into my mug and watch the powder swirling round, turning from a dusty nothing into sublime hot chocolate in seconds. All it takes is one extra element to transform it. I think about that every time I make hot chocolate.

Which is not a good thing, by the way. I think too much. Waaaay too much. Everyone's agreed on that.

"Try, at any rate," Frank says. "Please?"

"OK." I shrug, and take a sip of hot chocolate.

MY SERENE AND LOVING FAMILY—FILM TRANSCRIPT

INTERIOR. 5 ROSEWOOD CLOSE. DAY.

Mum, Dad and Frank are sitting round the breakfast
table. Mum is reading the *Mail*. Dad is on his
BlackBerry.

The camera zooms in on Frank. He looks thunderous and
sulky.

                         MUM
          So, Frank, what are you doing today
          after school?

Frank doesn't reply.

                         MUM
          Frank?

Frank is silent.

                         MUM
          FRANK?

She nudges Dad with her foot. Dad looks up,
bewildered.

                         MUM
          CHRIS!

She nods meaningfully at Frank. Dad cottons on.

                         DAD
          Frank, don't be so rude. We live in a
          family here. We communicate. Answer
          your mother.

                    FRANK
                 (rolls eyes)
        I don't know what I'm doing after
        school. Not playing computer games,
        clearly.

                    MUM
        Well, I want you to go through your
        shirts. I don't know what happens to
        them. Chris, we can go through yours too.

Dad is working on his BlackBerry.

                    MUM
        CHRIS? CHRIS?

Dad is too absorbed to hear.

                    FRANK
        Dad? Family? Communicate? Family?

He waves a hand in front of Dad's face and Dad finally
looks up. He blinks at Frank.

                    DAD
        No, you CANNOT go out tonight. You are
        grounded, young man.

He looks at the blank faces. Realizes he's got it wrong.

                    DAD
        I mean . . . stack the dishwasher.
                 (He tries again.)
        I mean, put your laundry in the right
        basket.
                 (gives up)
        Whatever your mother says.

It's the next night that Frank appears at the door of the den and says, with no preamble, "I'm going to bring Linus in to say hello."

"Right," I say, trying to sound relaxed and casual. "OK."

Relaxed and casual? What a joke. Already my whole body is tense. Already my breath is coming faster. Panic is rocketing round my body. I'm losing control. I hear Dr. Sarah's voice, and try to recall her soothing presence.

Allow the feelings to be there.

Acknowledge your lizard brain.

Reassure your lizard brain.

My damn lizard brain.

The thing about brains, which you might not know, is they're not just one ball of jelly. They're all divided up into bits, and some bits are great and some are just a waste of space. In my humble opinion.

So the one I could really do without is the lizard brain. Or the "amygdala," as it's called in the books. Every time you freeze in fright, that's your lizard brain taking over. It's called the lizard brain because we all had one of these even when we were lizards, apparently. It's, like, prehistoric. And it's really hard to control. I mean, OK, all bits of your brain are hard to control, but the lizard brain is the worst. It basically tells your body what to do through chemicals and electrical signals. It doesn't wait for evidence and it doesn't think, it just has instincts. Your lizard brain is *totally* not rational or reasonable: all it wants to do is protect you. Fight, flight, freeze.

So I can tell myself rationally that talking to Linus in the same room and everything will be fine. No worries. What's the problem? A conversation. What could be dangerous about a conversation?

But my stupid lizard brain is all, like, "Red alert! Danger! Run away! Panic! Panic!" And it's pretty loud and convincing. And my body tends to listen to *it*, not to me. So that's the bummer.

Every muscle in my body is taut. My eyes are flicking around in fear. If you saw me now you'd think there was a dragon in the room. My lizard brain is in overdrive. And even though I'm telling myself frantically to *ignore* the stupid lizard brain, it's kind of hard when you have a prehistoric reptile banging away inside your head, yelling "Run!"

"This is Linus." Frank's voice breaks into my thoughts. "I'll leave you two together."

And before I can escape, there he is, at the door. Same brown hair, same easy smile. I feel kind of unreal. All I can hear is my own brain saying *Don't run, don't run, don't run.*

"Hi," he says.

"Hi," I manage to reply.

The thought of facing him or looking at him is impossible, so I turn away. Right away. Staring into the corner.

"Are you OK?" Linus takes a few steps into the room and pauses.

"I'm fine."

"You don't look that fine," he ventures.

"Right. Well."

I pause, trying to think of an explanation that doesn't involve the words *weird* or *nutty*. "Sometimes I get too much adrenaline in my body," I say at last. "It's just, like, a thing. I breathe too fast, stuff like that."

"Oh, OK." I sense that he nods, although obviously, I can't *look* at him, so I can't be sure.

Simply sitting here and not running away feels like riding a rodeo. It's taking a major effort. My hands are twisting themselves up in knots. I have an aching desire to grab my T-shirt and start shredding it to bits, only I have vowed to Dr. Sarah that I will *stop* shredding my clothes. So I will not shred my top. Even though it would make me feel a ton better; even though my fingers are dying to find a place of safety.

"They should teach us this stuff in biology lessons," says Linus. "This is way more interesting than the life cycle of the amoeba. Can I sit down?" he adds awkwardly.

"Sure."

He perches on the edge of the sofa and, I can't help it, I edge away.

"Is this to do with everything that . . . happened?"

"A bit." I nod. "So you know about that."

"I just heard stuff. You know. Everyone was talking about it."

A sick feeling rises up inside me. How many times has Dr. Sarah said to me, "Audrey, everyone is not talking about you"? Well, she's wrong.

"Freya Hill's gone to my cousin's school," he continues. "I don't know what happened to Izzy Lawton or Tasha Collins."

I recoil at the names.

"I don't really want to talk about it."

"Oh. OK. Fair enough." He hesitates, then says, "So, you wear dark glasses a lot."

"Yeah."

There's a silence which I can sense he's waiting for me to fill.

And actually, why *not* tell him? If I don't, Frank probably will.

"I find eye contact hard," I admit. "Even with my family. It's too . . . I dunno. Too much."

"OK." He digests this for a moment. "Can you do anything contact? Do you email?"

"No." I swallow down a wince. "I don't do email at the moment."

"But you write notes."

"Yes. I write notes."

There's quiet for a moment; then a piece of paper arrives by my side, on the sofa. On it is written one word:

Hi.

I smile at it, and reach for a pen.

Hi.

I pass it back along the sofa. The next minute it appears again, and we're into a backwards and forwards conversation, all on paper.

Is this easier than talking?

A bit.

Sorry I mentioned your dark glasses. Sore point.

That's OK.

I remember your eyes from before.

Before?

I came round once to see Frank. I noticed your eyes then. They're blue, right?

I can't believe he registered the colour of my eyes.

Yes. Well remembered.

I'm sorry you have to go through all this.

Me too.

It won't be forever. You'll be in the dark for as long as it takes and then you'll come out.

I stare at what he's written, a bit taken aback. He sounds so confident.

You think?

My aunt grows special rhubarb in dark sheds. They keep it dark and warm all winter and harvest it by candlelight and it's the best stuff. She sells it for a fortune, btw.

So what, I'm rhubarb?

Why not? If rhubarb needs time in the dark maybe you do too.

I'm RHUBARB?!

There's a long pause. Then the paper arrives back under my nose. He's done a drawing of a rhubarb stalk with dark glasses on. I can't help a snort of laughter.

"So, I'd better go." He gets to his feet.

"OK. Nice to . . . you know. Chat."

"Same. Well, bye, then. See you soon."

I lift a hand, my face twisted resolutely away, desperately wishing I could turn towards him, telling myself to turn—but not turning.

They talk about "body language," as if we all speak it

the same. But everyone has their own dialect. For me right now, for example, swiveling my body right away and staring rigidly at the corner means, "I like you." Because I didn't run away and shut myself in the bathroom.

I just hope he realizes that.

At my next appointment with Dr. Sarah, she watches my documentary so far, while making notes. Mum has come to the appointment, as she does every now and then, and she keeps up a running commentary:

"I don't know WHAT I was wearing that day ... Dr. Sarah, please don't think our kitchen is usually that untidy ... Audrey, why did you film the compost heap, for goodness' sake"—until Dr. Sarah politely tells her to shut up. At the end she sits back in her chair and smiles at me.

"I enjoyed that. You've been a good fly on the wall, Audrey. Now I want that fly to buzz around the room a bit. Interview your family. Maybe some outsiders too. Push yourself a little."

At the word *outsiders* I clench up.

"What kind of outsiders?"

"Anyone. The milkman. Or one of your old school

friends?" She says this casually, as though she doesn't know that my "old school friends" are a sore point. For a start, what "old school friends"? There weren't that many to begin with, and I haven't seen any of them since leaving Stokeland.

Natalie was my best friend. She wrote me a letter after I left school and her mum sent flowers and I know they call Mum every so often. I just can't reply. I can't see her. I can't face her. And it doesn't help that Mum kind of blames Natalie for what happened. Or at least, she thinks Natalie was "culpable" for "not acting sooner." Which is so unfair. None of it was Natalie's fault.

I mean, yes, Natalie could have said something. The teachers might have believed me sooner then. But you know what? Natalie was paralysed by stress. And I get that now. I really do.

"So you'll do that, Audrey?" Dr. Sarah has this way of pressing you until you agree to do something, and she writes it down like homework and you can't pretend it doesn't exist.

"I'll try."

"Good! You need to start widening your horizons. When we suffer prolonged anxiety, we have a tendency to become self-obsessed. I don't mean that in a pejorative way," she adds. "It's simply a fact. You believe the whole world is thinking about you constantly. You believe the world is judging you and talking about you."

"They *are* all talking about me." I seize the opportunity to prove her wrong. "Linus told me they were. So."

Dr. Sarah looks up from her notes and gives me that pleasant, level look of hers.

"Who's Linus?"

"A boy. A friend of my brother."

Dr. Sarah is looking back at her notes.

"It was Linus who visited before? When you found things difficult?"

"Yes. I mean, he's OK, actually. We've talked."

A pink tinge is creeping over my face. If Dr. Sarah notices it, she doesn't say anything.

"He's a computer game addict, like Frank," says Mum. "Dr. Sarah, *what* am I going to do about my son? I mean, should I bring him to see you? What's normal?"

"I suggest we concentrate on Audrey today," says Dr. Sarah. "Feel free to consult me at a different time about Frank if you feel it would be helpful. Let's return to your concern, Audrey." She smiles at me, effectively dismissing Mum.

I can see Mum bristle, and I know she'll slag off Dr. Sarah a little in the car on the way home. Mum and Dr. Sarah have a weird relationship. Mum adores Dr. Sarah, like we all do, but I think she resents her too. I think she's secretly poised for the moment when Dr. Sarah says, *Well, Audrey, of course it's all the fault of your parents.*

Which of course Dr. Sarah never has said. And never will.

"The truth is, Audrey," Dr. Sarah is saying, "that yes, people will probably talk about you for a fraction of the time. I'm sure my patients talk about me, and I'm sure it's not always complimentary. But they'll get bored and move on. Can you believe that?"

"No," I say honestly, and Dr. Sarah nods.

"The more you engage with the outside world, the more you'll be able to turn down the volume on those worries. You'll see that they're unfounded. You'll see that the world is a very busy and varied place and most people have the attention span of a gnat. They've already forgotten what happened. They don't think about it. There will have been five more sensations since your incident. Won't there?"

I shrug reluctantly.

"But it's hard for you to believe that, trapped in your own little world. And for that reason, I'd like you to start making visits out of the house."

"What?" My chin jerks up in horror. "Where?"

"To your local high street?"

"No. I can't."

My chest has started to rise and fall at the very idea, but Dr. Sarah ignores it.

"We've talked about exposure therapy. You can start with a tiny visit. A minute or two. But you need to gradually expose yourself to the world, Audrey. Or the danger is, you really will become trapped."

"But . . ." I swallow, unable to talk properly. "But . . ."

There are black dots in front of my eyes. Dr. Sarah's room was always a safe space, but now I feel as though she's thrusting me into a pit of fire.

"Those girls might be anywhere," says Mum, protectively grabbing my hand. "What if she bumps into one of them? Two of them are still at school in the area, you know. I mean, it's outrageous. They should have been sent away. And when I say away, I mean *away*."

"I know it's difficult." Dr. Sarah is focused solely on me.

85

"I'm not suggesting you go out alone. But I think it's time, Audrey. I think you can do it. Call it Project Starbucks."

Starbucks? Is she *kidding*?

Tears have started to my eyes. My blood is pulsing in panic. I can't go to Starbucks. I can't.

"You're a brave, strong girl, Audrey," says Dr. Sarah, as though reading my mind, and she passes me a tissue. "You need to start pushing yourself. Yes you can."

◆ ◆ ◆

No I can't.

The next day I spend twelve solid hours in bed. Just the thought of Starbucks has sent me slithering down a tunnel of fear, to the black, dark place. Even the air seems abrasive. Every noise makes me flinch. I can't open my eyes.

Mum brings me soup and sits on my bed and strokes my hand.

"It's too soon," she says. "Too soon. These doctors get carried away. You'll get there in your own time."

My own time, I think after she's gone. What's that? What's Audrey time? Right now it feels like a slow-motion pendulum. It's lurching forwards and back, forwards and back, but the clock's not ticking round. I'm not getting anywhere.

And then three days have passed and the darkness has lifted and I'm out of bed, having an argument with Frank.

"Those were my Shreddies. I always eat Shreddies. You know that."

"No you don't," I say, to be annoying. "Sometimes you eat pancakes."

Frank looks like he might spontaneously combust.

"I eat pancakes *when Mum makes pancakes.* When she doesn't, I eat Shreddies. Every morning for the last five years. Ten years. And you just go and finish the packet."

"Have muesli."

"*Muesli?*" He looks so aghast at the idea, I want to giggle. "Like raisins and shit?"

"It's healthy."

"You don't even like Shreddies," he says accusingly. "Do you? You only took them to wind me up."

"They're OK." I shrug. "Not as good as muesli."

"I give up." Frank rests his head on his hands. "You're just *trying* to ruin my life." He shoots me a dark look. "I preferred you lying in bed."

"Well, I preferred you plugged into a computer," I shoot back. "You were much less of a pain when we never saw you."

"Frank!" As Mum bursts into the kitchen, holding Felix on one hip, she looks shocked at the sight of him, collapsed on the table. "Sweetheart. Are you OK?"

"Shreddies!" Felix yells as soon as he sees my bowl. "I want Shreddies! Please," he adds sweetly as he slithers down from Mum. "Please may I."

"Here you are." I pass the bowl to Felix. "You just had to ask nicely," I inform Frank. "Try learning from your brother."

Frank doesn't move a muscle. Mum comes over and prods him.

"Frank? Darling? Can you hear me?"

"I'm fine." At last he lifts his head, looking wan and pale. "Tired."

Now that I look at him, he does have black shadows under his eyes. "I think I've been overdoing it," he says weakly. "Homework and everything."

"Are you sleeping well?" Mum peers at him anxiously. "You teenagers need sleep. You should be sleeping fourteen hours a night."

"Fourteen hours?" We both stare at her.

"Mum, even comatose people don't sleep fourteen hours a night," says Frank.

"Ten hours, then," she amends. "Something. I'll look it up. Are you taking vitamins?"

Mum starts randomly pulling vitamin bottles out of the

cupboard. TeenVit, KidVit, Well Woman, Osteocare ... I mean, it's a joke. None of us ever takes them.

"Here." She plonks about ten capsules in front of Frank and another load in front of me. "Felix, sweetheart, come and have some magnesium."

"Don't want nesium!" he yells, and hides under the kitchen table. "No nesium!" He clamps his hands over his mouth.

"Oh, for God's sake." Mum swallows the magnesium pill herself, and sprays herself with something called Skin Enhancer, which has been sitting in the kitchen cupboard for three years, I know for a fact.

"You need some iron," she adds to Frank. "And an early night. I've got a DVD planned for this evening, which we can all watch, and then straight to bed."

"That sounds super-fun," says Frank, staring blankly into the middle distance.

"It's a classic," adds Mum. "Dickens."

"Dickens. Right." Frank shrugs like, *Who cares?*

"At least we've got you off those wretched computer games!" says Mum, sounding a bit too bright. "It just shows, you don't *need* to play them, do you? I mean, you've barely noticed, have you?"

"Barely noticed?" Frank finally lifts his gaze to meet hers. "Barely noticed? Are you joking? *Barely noticed?*"

"Well, it's not like you're counting down the days until—"

Mum stops abruptly as Frank lifts his sleeve to reveal a digital watch strapped to his arm.

"Sixty-one hours, thirty-four minutes, twenty-seven seconds till the ban is lifted," he says tonelessly. "I'm not just counting down, all my friends are counting down. So yes, Mum, I have 'noticed.' "

Frank can be pretty sarcastic when he wants to, and I see two little red spots appear on Mum's cheeks.

"Well, I don't care!" she snaps. "Tonight we're all going to watch *Great Expectations,* as a family, and believe it or not, Frank, you'll be amazed. You children think you know it all, but Dickens was one of the greatest storytellers ever, and you will be blown away by this film."

As she strides off again, Frank slumps down further on the kitchen table.

"You are so lucky," he says indistinctly. "No-one's on your case. You can do what the hell you like."

"I can't do what the hell I like!" I say defensively. "I have to do this documentary the whole time. And now I'm supposed to go to Starbucks."

"Why Starbucks?"

"Dunno. Starbucks therapy. Whatever."

"Right." Frank sounds supremely uninterested. But then, all of a sudden, he sits up. "Hey. Can you tell your therapist you'll be cured if you attend this year's European Gaming Expo in Munich and you have to take your brother?"

"No."

"Phhhmph." Frank subsides onto the table again. Mum's right, he does look rough.

"You can have these." I give him the last remaining dregs of Shreddies, which Felix has abandoned.

"Yeah, right. Soggy, third-hand Shreddies covered in Felix dribble. Thanks, Audrey." Franks gives me a death stare.

Then, a moment later, he reaches for a spoon and starts shoveling them in.

INTERIOR. 5 ROSEWOOD CLOSE. DAY.

Camera pans around the living room. It is in semi-
darkness. Mum is gazing raptly at the TV. Dad is
surreptitiously on his BlackBerry. Frank is staring at
the ceiling.

Music crashes from the TV. The camera pans to the TV
screen. Black-and-white writing reads "The End."

> **MUM**
> There! Wasn't that amazing? Wasn't it
> just the most gripping story?

> **FRANK**
> It was all right.

> **MUM**
> "All right"? Darling, it was DICKENS.

> **FRANK**
> (patiently)
> Yeah. It was Dickens and it was all right.

> **MUM**
> Well, it was better than one of your inane
> computer games, you have to admit that.

> **FRANK**
> No it wasn't.

> **MUM**
> Of course it was.

> **FRANK**
> It wasn't.

                              MUM
                           (erupts)
            Are you telling me that your ridiculous
            games can compete with a classic Dickens
            story? I mean, take the characters!
            Take Magwitch! Magwitch is unique!

                             FRANK
                        (unimpressed)
            Yeah, there's a Magwitch character in
            LOC too. Only he has, like, a better
            backstory than the Dickens one. He's
            a convict, the same, but he can help
            any competitor.

                     AUDREY (VOICE-OVER)
            He transfers powers.

                             FRANK
            Except the competitor has to take on
            one of his crimes and pay the penalty—

                         AUDREY (V.O.)
            Exactly. So you have to choose which
            power structure to go in at. And—

                             FRANK
            Shut up, Aud! I'm explaining. Except
            you don't know which penalty you've
            got till they make the choice. So it's
            like a gamble, only the more you play,
            the more you can work it out. It's
            awesome.

        Mum is looking from Frank to Audrey and back again, in
        total bafflement.

                               92

                    MUM

     OK, this makes no sense to me. None.
     What power structures? What is that?

                   FRANK

     If you played, you'd find out.

                AUDREY (V.O.)

     Magwitch *is* a pretty amazing character.

                    MUM

     Exactly! Thank you.

A slight pause.

                    MUM

     The Dickens Magwitch or the *LOC*
     Magwitch?

                AUDREY (V.O.)

     The *LOC* Magwitch, of course.

                   FRANK

     The Dickens one is just a bit . . .

                    MUM
                  (sharply)
     What? What's wrong with the Dickens
     Magwitch? What could be wrong with one
     of the great literary characters of
     our time?

                   FRANK

     He's less interesting.

                AUDREY (V.O.)

     Exactly.

                      93

                         FRANK
Two-dimensional.

                    AUDREY (V.O.)
I mean, he doesn't DO anything.

                         FRANK
                       (kindly)
No offense. I'm sure Dickens was a
great guy.

                          MUM
                      (to DAD)
Are you hearing this?

Mum's been pissed off with us ever since Dickensgate. She made us tidy our rooms today, which hardly ever happens, and she found a cheeseburger in Frank's room and it all kicked off.

I don't mean a cheeseburger carton, I mean an actual cheeseburger. He'd taken about two bites and put it back into the box and left it on the floor, like weeks ago. It was buried under a pile of rank sports kit. The weird thing is, the cheeseburger didn't moulder. It kind of fossilized. It was pretty gross.

Mum started on the hugest lecture about rats and vermin and hygiene, but Frank waved her away and said, "I have to go, Mum, Linus is like a minute away. You always say we have to be polite to guests and greet them." He stomped downstairs and I felt a bit swoopy in my stomach.

Linus again. I didn't think we'd be seeing so much of Linus while Frank was banned from computers.

Mum obviously thought the same thing, because she looked a bit thrown and called down the stairs, "He does know about your computer ban, doesn't he?" and Frank said impatiently, "Of course." Then he added, as he swung round into the hall, "But Linus can play *LOC* on my computer while he's here, can't he?"

Mum looked a bit flummoxed. She opened her mouth, but nothing came out. A moment later she was heading off to her bedroom, saying, "Chris? Chris, what do you think of this?"

That was all about ten minutes ago. I know Linus is here because I heard him arrive, a few minutes ago. He went straight into the playroom with Frank and I guess they fired up *LOC* straightaway. Meanwhile, I could hear Mum and Dad in discussion in their bedroom.

"It's the principle!" Mum kept saying. "He's got to learn!"

I think Dad was on the "They're only kids, it's all fairly harmless" tack and Mum was on the "Screens are evil and corrupting my son" tack, and they couldn't agree, so after a while I got bored listening. I headed down to the den and here I am now, waiting.

No, not waiting.

Well, kind of waiting.

I put on an old episode of *How I Met Your Mother* and try not to calculate how long a game of *LOC* is, and whether Linus might come and say hello when he's done. Just the thought of him is giving me little twinges. Good twinges. I think.

I mean, not that he *needs* to say hello. It's probably the last thing he wants to do. Why would he?

Only, he did say "See you soon." Why would he say "See you soon" if he was planning to ignore me for the rest of my life?

My hands are twisted up, and I try to unclench them. He won't come. He's here to see Frank, not me. I need to stop thinking about this. I turn up *How I Met Your Mother* and am flicking through a copy of *Closer* too, for good measure, when Felix comes charging towards the sofa.

"This pocket paper is for *you*!" he announces, and thrusts a piece of A4 at me.

Hi, Rhubarb.

He's drawn the picture of rhubarb in dark glasses again, and I feel my mouth twitch into a smile.

Hi, Orange Slice.

I'm terrible at drawing, but somehow I manage a picture of a face with hair and an orange segment for a mouth. I send Felix trotting off with it, and wait.

A few moments later I hear Mum and Dad coming down the stairs, and some sort of kerfuffle coming from the play-room.

"You are SO UNREASONABLE!" Frank's voice suddenly echoes though the house.

"PLEASE DO NOT SHOUT AT ME IN FRONT OF YOUR FRIENDS!" Mum shrieks back.

I instinctively have my hands over my ears and am

wondering whether to escape upstairs to my room, when there's a noise at the door. I look up—and it's him. It's Linus.

Before I know it, I've bolted into the furthest corner of the sofa.

Stupid, dumb lizard brain.

I stare fixedly at the wall and mutter, "Hi."

"Hi, Rhubarb. So what's this 'orange slice' thing?"

"Oh." I can't help a tiny smile, and my fists unclench a teeny smidgen. "I think your smile looks like an orange segment."

"My mum says it's like a crescent moon."

"There you go, then."

He moves a little into the room. I'm not looking that way, but my radar is on full twitch alert. If you spend most of your time turned away from people, you get to know what they're doing without having to see it.

"So—aren't you playing?" My voice comes out a little husky.

"Your mum's banned me. She got a bit mad. Frank was helping me play, and she started on this thing about how he was banned, and that included sitting with his friends, telling them what to do."

"Right." I nod. "I can imagine. Do your parents get so stressed about computer games?"

"Not really," says Linus. "They're more stressed about my granny. She lives with us and she's proper crazy. I mean—"

He stops abruptly and there's a prickly silence. It takes me about three seconds to realize why.

That's what he thinks I am, hits me with a horrible thud, followed by, *Of course he does.*

The silence is getting worse. I can sense the word *crazy* floating around in the air, like the words on Frank's French vocab program.

Crazy.

Fou.

I learned that in French, before I quit school. *Folie.* That means crazy too, doesn't it? Only it sounds like a chic form of crazy. Crazy in, like, a Breton-striped top with red lipstick.

"I'm sorry," says Linus.

"Don't be sorry," I say, almost aggressively. "You didn't say anything."

Which is true. He didn't say anything. He stopped midsentence.

Except that stopping midsentence is the worst thing people can do. It's like, totally passive-aggressive, because you can't take issue with anything they've said. You have to take issue with *what you think they were going to say.*

Which then they deny.

The Queen of the Midsentence Stop is my mum. I mean, she's an expert. Some recent examples in no particular order:

1.

MUM: Well, I really think your so-called friend Natalie could have—

Midsentence Stop.

ME: What? Prevented everything from happening? So it's her fault? We can lay everything at the door of Natalie Dexter?

MUM: Don't overreact, Audrey. I wasn't
going to *say* that.

2.

MUM: I've bought you some facial wash.
Look, it's especially formulated for teenage
skin.

ME (reading label): "For problem skin
breakouts." You think I have problem
skin?

MUM: Of course not, darling. But you
have to admit that sometimes it's a little—

Midsentence Stop.

ME: What? Rank? Gross? Like, I should
walk around with a bag over my head?

MUM: Don't overreact, Audrey. I wasn't
going to *say* that.

Anyway, so I'm quite attuned to the Midsentence Stop.
And Linus just stopped, totally midsentence, and I know
what he was going to say. He was going to say: *she's crazy
like you're crazy.*

He's repulsed by me. I knew it. He's only come by here
because it's like entertainment, like a freak show. The girl
in the dark glasses, roll up, roll up, see her cower in the
corner.

The silence is going on and on, and someone has to break
it, so I say tightly,

"It's fine. I'm crazy. Whatever."

"No!" Linus sounds really shocked. Shocked, embarrassed, discomfited. Kind of mortified. Like he can't believe I would say that. (I'm getting all this from one syllable, you understand.)

"You're nothing like my granny," he adds, and he gives this little laugh, like he's enjoying a private joke. "If you met her you'd understand."

Linus's voice is kind of easy. Not like Frank's, which sounds like a harsh battering ram most of the time. He laughs again and I feel like this swooshing of relief. If he can laugh, then he's not repulsed, right?

"So I guess I won't be round again till Frank's ban is lifted."

"Right."

"Your mum thinks I'm a bad influence."

"My mum thinks *everything* is a bad influence." I roll my eyes, even though he can't see.

"So do you ever go out or anything?"

He hasn't stopped midsentence, but still the air feels prickly. At least, the air around me feels prickly. *Go out or anything.* I feel an urge to curl up and shut my eyes.

"No. Not really."

"Right."

"I mean, I'm supposed to go to Starbucks."

"Awesome. When are you going to go?"

"I'm not." I say it roughly, without even meaning to. "It's . . . I can't."

There's another silence. I'm hunched away even further. I can sense his questions circulating around the silence like more vocab words: *Why? How come? What's going on?*

"I'm supposed to do, like, exposure therapy," I say in a

miserable rush. "Like, you do a little bit at a time. But Star-bucks isn't a little bit. It's huge. I just can't. So."

With every revelation, I'm expecting him to leave. But he's still here.

"Like allergies," he says, sounding fascinated. "Like, you're allergic to Starbucks."

"I guess." This conversation is starting to wear away at my brain. I'm clutching a cushion for comfort; the tendons are standing up on my hands.

"So you're allergic to eye contact."

"I'm allergic to everything contact."

"No you're not," he says at once. "You're not allergic to *brain* contact. I mean you write notes. You talk. You still want to talk to people, you just can't. So your body needs to catch up with your brain."

I'm silent for a while. No-one's put it like that before.

"I suppose," I say at last.

"What about shoe contact?"

"What?"

"Shoe contact!"

"What's *shoe* contact?" I'd laugh, only my stupid lizard brain has disabled the laugh button for now. I'm too frozen up with tension.

I am owed so much laughter. Sometimes I hope I'm building up a stockpile of missing laughs, and when I've recovered, they'll all come exploding out in one gigantic fit that lasts twenty-four hours.

Meanwhile, Linus has sat down on the sofa, at the other end from me. In my peripheral vision I see him extending a grubby trainer.

"Go on," he says. "Shoe contact. Let's do it."

I can't move. I'm a hedgehog rolled into a ball. I don't want to know.

"You can move your foot," says Linus. "You don't have to look at it. Just move it."

He sounds persistent. I can't believe this is happening. My lizard brain is *really* not liking this. It's telling me to dive under the blanket. Hide. Run. Anything.

Maybe if I don't react, I tell myself, *he'll just give up and we can forget all about it.*

But the seconds tick on, and he doesn't go anywhere.

"Go on," he says encouragingly. "I bet you can do it."

And now I have Dr. Sarah's voice in my head: *You need to start pushing yourself.*

Gradually, I shift my foot across the carpet, until the rubber rim of my trainer is touching the rubber rim of his. The rest of my body is still turned away. I'm staring fixedly at the fabric of the sofa, my entire brain focused on the inch of foot that is in contact with his.

And OK, I know there's like two layers of trainer rubber between us, I know this could not be less erotic or romantic or whatever, and by the way, my entire body is still twisted firmly away from his as if I can't stand the sight of him. But still, it feels kind of—

Well.

See how I stopped midsentence? I can do it too. When I don't necessarily want to reveal the *exact* thought I'm having.

I feel breathless, is all I will admit to.

"There." He sounds satisfied. "See?"

Linus doesn't sound breathless. He just sounds interested, like I proved a point which now he'll tell his friends about or write up in his blog or whatever. He leaps to his feet and says, "So, I'll see you," and the spell is broken.

"Yeah. See you."

"Your mum will chase me out of the house in a minute. I'd better go."

"Huh. Yeah."

I hunch towards the sofa corner, determined not to give away how I kind of wish he'd stay.

"Oh. Um," I say as he reaches the door. "Maybe I could interview you for my documentary."

"Oh yeah?" He pauses. "What's that?"

"I have to make this documentary, and I'm supposed to interview people who come to the house, so . . ."

"OK. Cool. Whenever. I'll be back after . . . you know. When Frank can play games again."

"Cool."

He disappears and I stay motionless for a while, wondering if he'll come back or send me any more notes, or a message via Frank or whatever.

Which of course he doesn't.

MY SERENE AND LOVING FAMILY—FILM TRANSCRIPT

INTERIOR. 5 ROSEWOOD CLOSE. DAY.

The camera approaches the door of the study. It
edges inside. Dad is sitting at his desk. His eyes
are closed. On his screen is a different Alfa
Romeo car.

> **AUDREY (VOICE-OVER)**
> Dad? Are you asleep?

Dad jumps and opens his eyes.

> **DAD**
> Of course I'm not asleep. Just
> working here. Getting some work
> done.

He moves his mouse and clicks off the Alfa Romeo car.

> **AUDREY (V.O.)**
> I'm supposed to interview you.

> **DAD**
> Great! Fire away.

He swivels his chair round to face the camera and
gives a cheesy smile.

> **DAD**
> The life and times of Chris Turner,
> accountant to the stars.

> **AUDREY (V.O.)**
> No you're not.

Dad looks defensive.

> ### DAD
> OK, accountant to several medium-sized
> firms, one in media. I do get tickets
> to concerts.

> ### AUDREY (V.O.)
> I know.

> ### DAD
> And you all met those TOWIE people,
> remember? At the Children in Need event?

> ### AUDREY (V.O.)
> It's OK, Dad, I think your job is cool.

> ### DAD
> You could ask me about my rowing at
> college.

He casually flexes a bicep.

> ### DAD
> Still got it. Or you could ask me about
> my band.

> ### AUDREY (V.O.)
> Right. Yes. The . . . Turtles?

> ### DAD
> The Moonlit Turtles. Moonlit. I gave
> you the CD, remember?

> ### AUDREY (V.O.)
> Yes! It's great, Dad.

Dad has an idea. He points at the camera, almost
speechless with excitement.

                    DAD

     I have it! You want a sound track for
     your film? I can give you one, free of
     charge. Original music, performed by
     the Moonlit Turtles, one of the most
     exciting student acts of the 1990s!

                  AUDREY (V.O.)
     Right.
                    (pause)
     Or I could choose my own music . . .

                    DAD

     No! Sweetheart, I want to HELP. This
     way we work together. It'll be a family
     project. It'll be fun! I'll buy the
     software, we'll edit it together, you
     can choose your favourite songs . . .

He has called up a playlist on his computer.

                    DAD

     Let's have a listen now. Tell me your
     favourite song, we'll put it on, play
     around.

                  AUDREY (V.O.)
     My favourite song of all time?

                    DAD
     No! Your favourite song by the Moonlit
     Turtles. Your favourite song that your
     old Dad performs in. You must have one?
     A favourite?

Long pause. Dad looks at the camera expectantly.

                              DAD

          You told me you listened to the CD over
          and over on your iPod.

                         AUDREY (V.O.)
                           (quickly)
          I did! All the time. So. Um. Favourite
          song. There are so many.
                            (pause)
          I think it would have to be . . .
          the loud one.

                              DAD

          Loud one?

                         AUDREY (V.O.)
          The one with the . . . um. Drums. It's
          really good.

The camera starts to back away as a heavy rock track
powers through the room. Dad is nodding his head
along.

                              DAD

          This one?

                         AUDREY (V.O.)
          Yes! Exactly! It's great. So good. Dad,
          I have to go . . .

The camera retreats out of the room.

                         AUDREY (V.O.)
          Oh God.

As I go to bed that night I'm thinking about Linus, I'm trying to picture myself greeting him at the front door when he comes round next. Like other people do. Normal people. I mean, I know how the script should go:

"Hey, Linus."

"Hey, Audrey."

"How's it been going?"

"Yeah, good."

Maybe a high five. Maybe a hug. Definitely a pair of smiles.

I can think of about sixty-five reasons why this is not going to happen any time soon. But it might, mightn't it? It *might*?

Dr. Sarah says positive visualization is an incredibly effective weapon in our armory and I should create in my mind scenarios of success that are realistic and encouraging.

The trouble is, I don't know how realistic my ideal scenario is.

OK, yes I do: not at all.

In the ideal scenario, I don't have a lizard brain. Everything is easy. I can communicate like normal people. My hair is longer and my clothes are cooler, and in my last fantasy, Linus wasn't even at the front door, he was taking me on a picnic in a wood. I have no idea where *that* came from.

Anyway. The ban is over tomorrow. Linus will be round again. And we'll see.

Except I hadn't reckoned on the apocalypse, which hit our house at 3:43 this morning. I know, because that was the time I blinked awake and stared blearily at my clock, wondering if there was a fire. There was a distant high-pitched screaming noise, which could have been an alarm, or could have been a siren, and I grabbed my robe off the floor and shoved my feet into my furry slippers and thought in a panic *What do I take?*

I grabbed my ancient pink teddy and my picture of me with Granny before she died, and I was halfway down the stairs when I realized that the noise wasn't a siren. Or an alarm. It was Mum. I could hear her in the playroom, and she was screaming, "What are you DOING?"

I skittered to the entrance and felt my whole body sag in astonishment. Frank was sitting at his computer playing *LOC.* At 3:43 a.m.

I mean, obviously he wasn't playing *LOC* right that second. He'd paused. But the graphics were there on the screen, and his headset was on, and he was looking up at Mum like a cornered fox.

"What are you DOING?" Mum yelled again, then turned to Dad, who had just arrived at the doorway too. "What is he DOING? Frank, what are you DOING?"

Parents have this way of asking really dumb, obvious questions.

Are you going out in that skirt?

No, I'm planning to take it off as soon as I get out of the front door.

Do you think that's a good idea?

No, I think it's a terrible idea, that's why I'm doing it.

Are you listening to me?

Your voice is a hundred decibels, I can hardly avoid it.

"What are you DOING?" Mum was still shrieking, and Dad put a hand on her arm.

"Anne," he said. "Anne, I have an eight o'clock."

Big mistake. Mum turned on him like *he* was the baddie.

"I don't care about your eight o'clock! This is your *son*, Chris! Lying to us! Playing computer games at night! What else has he been doing?"

"I couldn't sleep," said Frank. "OK? That's all. I couldn't sleep and I thought, *I'll read a book*, but I couldn't find a book, so I thought I'd just . . . you know. Wind down."

"How long have you been up?" snapped Mum.

"Since about two?" Frank looked plaintively at her. "I couldn't sleep. I think I'm getting insomnia."

Dad yawned and Mum glared at him.

"Anne," he said. "Can we do this in the morning? It's not going to help Frank's insomnia if we all argue now. Please? Bed?" He yawned again, his hair all tufty like a teddy bear's. "Please?"

◆ ◆ ◆

So that was last night. And things have not been Happy Families today. Mum gave Frank the third degree over breakfast, about: How many times has he got up in the night to play *LOC*? and How long has he had insomnia? and Did he realize that computer games *give* people insomnia?

Frank barely answered. He looked pretty gaunt and pale and out of it. The more Mum went on about circadian rhythms and light pollution and Why didn't he drink Ovaltine before bed? the more he retreated into his Frank shell.

I don't even know what Ovaltine is. Mum always brings it up when she talks about sleep. She refers to it like it's some magic potion and says "Why don't we drink it?" but she's never bought any, so how can we?

So then Frank went off to school and I read *Game of Thrones* all morning and then fell asleep. This afternoon I've been filming some birds in the garden, which I sense is not what Dr. Sarah wants, but it's peaceful. They're very cute. They come and eat crumbs off the bird table and fight with each other. Maybe I'll become a wildlife photographer or filmmaker or whatever. The only downer is your knees start to ache from crouching. Also, I'm not sure who's going to watch an hour's footage of birds eating crumbs.

So I'm pretty zoned out, and I jump in surprise when I hear a car coming into the drive. It's too early for Dad, so who is it? Maybe someone gave Frank a lift home from school. That happens sometimes.

Maybe Linus.

I cautiously creep round the edge of the house and peek into the drive. To my surprise, it is Dad. He's getting out of his car in his business suit, looking a bit hassled. The next minute the front door has opened and Mum is coming down the path like she expected him.

"Chris! At last."

"I came as soon as I could get away. But you know, I have a lot on right now . . . Is this really essential?"

"Yes it is! This is a crisis, Chris. A crisis with our son. And I need your support!"

OMG. What happened?

I duck back into the garden and head silently into the kitchen, where I can hear them talking. I edge forward and see them coming into the hall.

"I took Frank's computer to my Pilates class," Mum is saying grimly.

"You did *what*?" Dad seems flummoxed. "Anne, I know you want to keep it away from Frank, but isn't that a bit extreme?"

I have visions of Mum, staggering into the church hall, holding Frank's computer, and I have to clamp my mouth tightly closed to stop laughing. Is she going to take Frank's computer everywhere now? Like a pet?

"You don't understand!" spits Mum. "I took it for Arjun to have a look at."

"Arjun?" Dad looks more baffled than ever.

"Arjun is in my Pilates class. He's a computer software

developer and he works from home. I said, 'Arjun, can you tell from this computer how often my son has been playing games during the last week?'"

"Right." Dad eyes her warily. "And could Arjun tell?"

"Oh, he could tell," says Mum in ominous tones. "He could tell, all right."

There's silence. I can see Dad instinctively backing away, but he can't escape before the tidal wave of sound hits him.

"Every night! EVERY NIGHT! He starts at two a.m. and he logs off at six. Can you believe it?"

"You're joking." Dad seems genuinely shocked. "Are you sure?"

"Ask Arjun." Mum proffers her phone. "Ask him! He does freelance work for Google. He knows what he's talking about."

"Right. No, it's fine. I don't need to talk to Arjun." Dad sinks onto the stairs. "Jesus. Every night?"

"He creeps around. Lies to us. He's addicted! I knew it. I *knew* it."

"OK. Well, that's it, he's banned for life."

"Life." Mum nods.

"Till he's an adult."

"At least," Mum says. "At least. You know, Alison at my book group doesn't even have TV in the house. She says screens are the cigarettes of our age. They're toxic, and we're only going to realize the damage they're doing when it's too late."

"Right." Dad looks uneasy. "I'm not sure we need to go that far, do we?"

"Well, maybe we should!" Mum cries, sounding stressed.

"You know, Chris, maybe we've got this all wrong! Maybe we should go back to basics. Card games. Family walks. Discussions."

"Er . . . OK."

"I mean, books! What happened to books? That's what we should be doing! Reading the Booker short list! Not watching all this toxic, mindless television and playing brain-sapping video games. I mean, what are we doing, Chris? What are we *doing*?"

"Absolutely." Dad is nodding fervently. "No, I totally agree. Totally agree." There's a slight pause before he says, "What about *Downton*?"

"Oh, well, *Downton*." Mum looks wrong-footed. "That's different. That's . . . you know. History."

"And *The Killing*?"

My parents are addicted to *The Killing*. They gorge themselves on like four episodes at a time, and then say, "One more? Just one more?"

"I'm talking about the *children*," says Mum at last. "I'm talking about the *future generation*. They should be reading books."

"Oh, good." Dad exhales in relief. "Because whatever else I do in my life, I'm finishing *The Killing*."

"Are you kidding? We have to finish *The Killing*," Mum agrees. "We could watch one tonight."

"We could watch two."

"After we've spoken to Frank."

"Oh God." Dad rubs his head. "I need a drink."

◆ ◆ ◆

The house is quiet for a while after that. It's the calm before the kickoff. Felix comes home from a playdate where they made pizza and unveils the most revolting tomatoey-cheesy mess and makes Mum heat it up in the oven. Then he refuses to eat it.

Then he refuses to eat anything else, because he wants to eat the pizza he made, *even though he won't eat it.* I know. The logic of a four-year-old is beyond weird.

"I want to eat MY pizza!" he keeps wailing, whereupon Mum says, "Well, eat it, then! Here it is."

"Nooo!" He gazes at it tearfully. "Nooo! Not that one! Not THAT one!"

Eventually he swipes it off the table altogether, and seeing it collapsed on the floor is too much for him. He descends into hysterical sobbing and Mum says darkly, "They probably gave him Fruit Shoots," and hauls him off for a bath. (Half an hour later he's all fluffy and clean and smiling and eating sandwiches. Baths are like Valium for four-year-olds.)

Then I'm put on make-sure-Felix-eats-his-crusts duty, so I'm stuck at the kitchen table. I kind of thought I might get to Frank first and warn him. But it probably wouldn't have worked anyway, because Mum's like a sentry on speed. She goes into the hall every five minutes and opens the front door, and once she actually goes into the street, scanning the horizon all around, as if Frank might fool her by coming from some different direction. She's pretty revved up for seeing him. She keeps addressing the hall mirror with phrases like "It's the *deceit* as much as anything else" and "Yes, this *is* tough love. It *is* tough love, young man."

Young man.

Meanwhile I've kept my head well down, although I'm dying to ask Frank whether he's really been getting up at two a.m., and whether Linus was playing with him. I'm just secretly eating a couple of Felix's crusts for him, to speed things up, when I hear a yell from Mum. She's out in the front drive squinting along the road.

"Chris! Chris! He's coming!" She comes striding into the house, her head swiveling around on full alert. "Where's your father? Where's he gone?"

"Dunno. Haven't seen him."

OK, Mum's totally wired. I wonder whether I should tell her about breathing in for four counts and out for seven, but I think she'd bite my head off.

"Chris!" She stalks out of the kitchen.

I creep forward so I have a view of the hall. I should really get my video camera, only it's upstairs, and I don't want to venture across the battlefield. Dad appears at his study door, holding his BlackBerry to his ear, pulling an agonised face at Mum.

"Yes, the figures *were* unexpected," he's saying. "But if you look at page six ..." *Sorry,* he mouths at Mum. *Two minutes.*

"Great!" she snaps as Dad disappears again. "So much for a united front." She peers out of the hall window. "OK. Here he comes. Here we go."

She positions herself in the hall, her hand placed on her hip and glary eyes focused right on the door. After a tense ten seconds the door opens and I catch my breath. Frank saunters in, just the same as usual, and looks at Mum without much interest. I can see her draw herself up and take a deep breath.

"Hello, Frank," she says in steely tones, which make me shiver, even though I'm not the one in trouble. But Frank has his earphones in, so I'm guessing he didn't pick up on the steely tones.

"Hi," he says, and makes to go past, but Mum pokes him on the shoulder.

"Frank!" she says, and gestures to his ears. "Out!"

Rolling his eyes, Frank takes out his earphones and looks at her. "What?"

"So," says Mum, in yet more steely tones.

"What?

"So."

I can see her aim is to make him quake in fear with just that one syllable, but it hasn't really worked. He just looks impatient.

"So? What do you mean? So what?"

"We've been expecting you, Frank. Dad and I." She takes a step forward, her eyes like lasers. "We've been waiting for you for *quite a while*."

OMG. She's totally channelling a Bond villain, I realize. I bet she wishes she had a white cat to stroke.

"What's my computer doing there?" Frank suddenly notices it, perched on the hall table with its flex coiled around the plug.

"Good question," says Mum pleasantly. "Would you like to tell us about your computer activity over the last week or so?"

Frank's shoulders sag, like *Not this again.*

"I was playing *LOC*," he says in a monotone. "You caught me."

"Just the once?"

Frank lets his school bag slither to the ground.

"I dunno. I've got a headache. I need some paracetamol."

"And why would that be?" Mum suddenly loses it. "Would that be because you haven't had any sleep this week?"

"What?" Frank gives her his special, blank, I-have-no-idea-what-you're-talking-about look, which, actually, is really annoying.

"Don't play ignorant with me! Don't you dare play ignorant!" Mum is breathing really hard by now. "My friend Arjun looked at your machine today. And *what* an interesting story."

"Who's Arjun?" Frank scowls.

"A computer expert," says Mum triumphantly. "He told me all about you. You've left quite the trail, young man. We know everything."

I see a flicker of alarm pass across Frank's face. "Did he read my *emails*?"

"No. He didn't read your emails." Mum looks momentarily distracted. "What's in your emails?"

"Nothing," says Frank hastily, and glowers at her. "Jesus. I can't believe you hacked into my computer."

"Well, I can't believe you've been lying to us! You've been up at two a.m. every night this week! Do you deny it?"

Frank shrugs with a sullen expression.

"Frank?"

"If *Arjun* says it, it must be true."

"So it *is* true! Frank, do you understand how serious this is? *Do* you? DO YOU?" she suddenly yells.

"Well, do you understand how seriously I take *LOC*?" he yells back. "What if I become a professional gamer? What will you say then?"

"Not this again." Mum closes her eyes and massages her forehead. "Who were you playing with? Do I know them? Do I need to call their parents?"

"I doubt it," says Frank sarcastically, "since they live in Korea."

"*Korea?*" This seems the last straw for Mum. "Right. That's it, Frank. You are banned. Banned, banned, banned. Forever. No computers. No screens. No nothing."

"OK," says Frank limply.

"Do you understand?" She stares at him, hard. "You're banned."

"I get it. I'm banned."

There's a silence. Mum seems dissatisfied. She's peering at Frank as though she wanted to hear something else.

"You're banned," she tries again. "For good."

"I know," says Frank with elaborate patience. "You told me."

"You're not reacting. Why aren't you reacting?"

"I *am* reacting, Mum. I'm banned. Whatever."

"I'm locking this computer right away."

"I get it."

There's another weird, tense silence. Mum is studying Frank closely, as though searching for the answer. Then suddenly her whole face seems to ping, and she draws breath.

"Oh my God. You don't take this seriously, do you?

You think you'll get round it. What, you're already planning how you'll creep around the house at night and find your computer?"

"No." Frank sounds sulky, which means *Yes.*

"You're already planning how you'll pick the lock?"

"No."

"You think you can beat us!" She's quivering now. "You think you can beat us, don't you? Well, *beat this!*"

She grabs the computer, which is pretty bulky, and heads up the stairs, trailing the cord.

"This is going. It's going! I want it out of our house! I want it in smithereens."

"Smithereens?" Frank springs to life.

"You're banned anyway, so what does it matter?" Mum shoots back over her shoulder.

"Mum, no," says Frank in a panic. "Mum, what are you doing?"

"You stay there, young man!" Mum's voice is suddenly on a whole different level. She sounds properly scary, like she did when we were little kids, and Frank pauses, his foot on the step. I've never seen him look so freaked.

"What's she going to do?" he says in a low voice.

"I dunno. But I wouldn't go upstairs."

"But what's she *doing*?"

At that moment Felix comes bounding into the hall from the garden, in his dressing gown.

"Guess what?" he says in tones of joy. "Mummy is *throwing the computer out of the window!*"

I can't believe she did it. I can't believe she actually chucked Frank's computer out of the window.

It wasn't *quite* as dramatic as it might have been, because she suddenly got all health and safety and shouted to the neighbours to get out of the way, and then said to Dad that he should move the car if he was that worried.

Meanwhile Frank was lurching between total gibbering panic and trying to be one of those guys in the movies who talk the terrorist out of setting off the bomb.

"Mum, listen," he kept saying. "Put the computer down. You don't want to do this, Mum."

Which didn't work. Mostly because she *did* want to do it.

The computer didn't actually smash into smithereens when she threw it. It kind of bounced twice and landed on its side. In fact, it barely looked broken at all, once it was sitting on the lawn. There was just a bit of shattered glass from the screen, which Dad immediately cleared up because of Felix playing outside in bare feet or whatever.

But I guess it's messed up enough inside that Frank can't use it anymore. It looked a bit sad, sitting on the grass with his ancient Minecraft stickers all over it.

Everyone stared at it for a while, and a couple of people took photos, and then they all drifted home. I mean, hand on heart, it was a bit of an anticlimax. But not for Frank. He's devastated. I tried to say "I'm sorry" as we went inside, and he couldn't even answer.

I think he's in shock. He hasn't really spoken all evening. Mum is grimly triumphant and I think Dad is just relieved that the car didn't get trashed.

And although I really don't want to get into it, I'm wondering one thing. Does this mean Linus won't come round anymore?

INTERIOR. 5 ROSEWOOD CLOSE. DAY.

Mum is sitting in the kitchen with a coffee cup, looking straight to camera.

> **MUM**
> I did the right thing. OK, it was a bit extreme. But sometimes you have to take extreme measures, and everyone's shocked, but afterwards they say, "Wow. That was really adventurous and farsighted of you."

Silence.

> **MUM**
> I mean, I KNOW I did the right thing. And yes, things are tense at the moment, but they'll get better. Of course Frank didn't react well, of course he's angry—what did I expect?

Silence.

> **MUM**
> Well, I didn't expect it would be as bad as this. To be honest. But we'll get through it.

Mum lifts her coffee cup, then puts it down without drinking.

> **MUM**
> The thing about being a parent, Audrey, is that it's no picnic.

You have to make difficult choices
and you have to see them through.
So yes, I'm finding Frank a little
challenging right at the moment.
But you know what? He'll thank
me one day.

Silence.

                    MUM
Well, he might thank me.

Silence.

                    MUM
OK, so the thanking is unlikely. But
the point is, I'm a mother. Mothers
don't run away when things get tough.

Camera pans to Mum's BlackBerry and focuses in on a
Google search:

   Spa breaks for single women, no children allowed

Mum hastily covers it with her hand.

                    MUM
That's nothing.

So Frank's basically not speaking anymore. To anyone.

Actually, I quite like a silent Frank. It's peaceful around the place. But it's stressing Mum out. She even spoke to his teacher at school, who was, according to her, "Useless! Worse than useless! He said Frank seemed 'fine' to him and we should 'let him alone.' 'Let him alone,' can you believe it?" (I know this because I was outside Mum's room while she was sounding off to Dad.)

Tonight he's sitting at supper, eating his enchiladas without looking at anyone, staring ahead like a zombie. When Mum or Dad ask him anything, like "Have you got much homework?" or "What happened today at school?" he just answers with a "Phrrrmph" noise, or rolls his eyes or ignores them.

I'm not feeling Ms. Chatty either tonight, so it's not the liveliest dinner table. In fact, we all look up in relief when Felix comes in from the playroom in his tractor pyjamas.

"I didn't do my homework," he says, looking worried. "My *homework,* Mummy."

He's holding out some kind of transparent folder with a sheet in it.

"Oh, for God's sake," says Mum.

"Homework?" says Dad. "For a four-year-old?"

"I know." Mum sighs. "It's nuts." She pulls out the sheet and it's a big photocopied page entitled *Why we love each other.* Under the heading, Felix has drawn what I assume is a picture of us. At least, there are five figures. Mum looks pregnant and Dad looks like a gnome. I have a head the size of a pin and twenty very large circular fingers. But, you know, apart from that it's pretty accurate.

" 'Fill in the box with help from your family,' " Mum reads. " 'For example, "We love each other because we give each other cuddles." ' " She reaches for a pen. "OK. What shall I put? Felix, what do you love about our family?"

"Pizza," says Felix promptly.

"We can't put pizza."

"Pizza!" wails Felix. "I love pizza!"

"I can't put, 'We love each other because of pizza.' "

"I think that's a pretty good answer," says Dad, shrugging.

"I'll do it," says Frank, grabbing the page, and we all look up in shock. Frank spoke! He takes a black Sharpie from his pocket and reads aloud as he writes:

" 'We love each other because we respect each other's choices and understand when a person has a hobby that they love, and would never deliberately damage their property.' Oh, wait."

"Frank, you can't write that!" says Mum sharply.

It's a bit late to say that, since he's already written it. In permanent ink.

"Great!" Mum glares at Frank. "So now you've ruined your brother's homework sheet."

"I've spoken the truth." Frank glowers back at her. "You can't handle the truth."

A Few Good Men," says Dad promptly. "I didn't know you'd seen that."

"YouTube." Frank gets to his feet and heads over to the dishwasher.

"Well, marvellous," says Mum, looking totally pissed off. "Now we can't send this in. I'll have to write a note in his link book. 'Dear Mrs. Lacy, unfortunately Felix's homework was . . .' what?"

"Chewed by rats," I suggest.

" 'Inapplicable to the Turner family as they do not understand the concept of love beyond their own self-serving version,'" comes Frank's sonorous voice from the sink.

As he slouches out of the kitchen, Mum and Dad exchange glances.

"That boy needs a hobby," mutters Mum. "We should never have let him give up the cello."

"Please not the cello again," says Dad, looking alarmed. "I think he's beyond the cello."

"I'm not saying the cello!" snaps Mum. "But something. What do teenagers do these days?"

"All sorts of things." Dad shrugs. "Win Olympic medals, get into Harvard, create Internet companies, star in blockbuster films . . ." As he trails off, he looks a bit depressed.

"He doesn't need to win a medal," says Mum firmly. "He just needs an interest. What about the guitar?" Her face brightens. "Can he still play that? Why don't you two jam together in the garage?"

"We tried that once," says Dad, pulling a face. "Remember? It wasn't a success . . . but we can try again!" he amends quickly, at Mum's expression. "Good idea! We'll have a bit of a jamming session. Father and son. We'll play some tracks, get in the beers—I mean, not the beers," he adds hastily as Mum opens her mouth. "No beers."

"And he should volunteer," says Mum with sudden determination. "Yes! *That's* what Frank can do. Volunteer."

◆ ◆ ◆

I'm sitting in the kitchen later that evening, fiddling with the playback on my camera, when Frank shuffles in.

"Oh, hi." I raise my head, remembering something. "Listen, I haven't interviewed you yet. Can we do it?"

"I don't want to be interviewed."

Frank looks like he hates everyone and everything. His face is pale. His eyes are bloodshot. He looks *less* healthy than when he was gaming all the time.

"OK." I shrug. I reach for a Dorito from the bowl still sitting on the table. We had Tex-Mex for supper tonight, which is the only time Mum buys crisps. It's like, if they're Doritos and scooping up guacamole then they don't count as junk food. "So . . ." I try to speak casually. "I was wondering . . ."

My voice is letting me down. It doesn't sound casual, it sounds over-alert. On the other hand, I don't think Frank is in a noticing mood.

"Is Linus coming over?" It comes out in a hurry and I sound the opposite of casual, but there you go. I've asked.

Frank turns his head to give me a murderous glare.

"Why would Linus come over?"

"Well ... because ..." I'm confused. "Have you had a fight?"

"No, I haven't had a fight." His eyes are so bleak and full of anger, I flinch. "I've been dropped from the team."

"Dropped from the team?" I stare at him in shock. "But it was your team."

"Well, I can hardly play now, can I?"

His voice is all muffled and low. I have a horrible feeling he wants to cry. I haven't seen Frank cry since he was about ten.

"Frank." I feel a huge wave of sorrow for him. In fact, I think I might cry for him instead. "Have you told Mum?"

"Told Mum?" he lashes out. "What, so she can stand there and cheer?"

"She wouldn't!" I say. But actually I'm not sure.

The thing about Mum is, she doesn't know what she's talking about. I don't mean that in a bad way. It's just, no adults do. They're totally ignorant, but they're in control. It's nuts. The parents are in charge of all the stuff like *technology in the house* and *time on screens* and *hours on social media,* but then their computer goes wrong and they're like a baby, going, "What happened to my document?" "I can't get Facebook." "How do I load a picture? Double-click what? What does that mean?"

And we have to sort it out for them.

So Mum probably *would* cheer if she heard Frank wasn't

on the team anymore. And then in the next breath she'd say, "Darling, why don't you take up a hobby and join a team?"

"I'm really sorry, Frank," I say, but he doesn't react. The next minute he's shuffled out of the kitchen and I'm left alone with the Doritos.

"So things haven't been good." Dr. Sarah sounds as un-ruffled as ever.

"They're OK. But everyone's stressy. I've been in bed a lot. It's like, I'm so *tired* all the time."

"When you're tired, just rest. Don't fight it. Your body's mending itself."

"I know." I sigh, my legs hunched up on the chair. "But I don't want to be tired. I don't want to be overwhelmed. I want to kick this."

The words come out before I've thought them, and I feel a sudden little jab of adrenaline.

When I say things to Dr. Sarah, it's as if I'm hearing them for the first time and suddenly they become real. She's a bit magic, I think. She's like a fortune-teller—only in the present, not the future. Things change in her room. I don't know how, they just do.

"Good!" she says. "That's good. But, Audrey, what you don't seem to realize is, you *are* kicking it."

"No I'm not." I look at her resentfully. How can she say that?

"You are."

"I've been in bed for, like, the last three days."

"No-one said getting better would be a straightforward journey. Remember our graph?"

She gets up and heads for her whiteboard. She draws two axes and a jagged red line heading up.

"You'll go up and you'll go down. But your progress will be in the right direction. It *is* in the right direction. You've come a long way, Audrey. Remember our first meeting?"

I shrug. Some of our sessions are a bit of a blur, to be honest.

"Well, I do. And believe me, I'm pleased with what I see before me today."

"Oh." I feel a tiny glow of pride, which is pathetic. I mean, I didn't *do* anything.

"How's the film going?"

"It's OK." I nod.

"Have you interviewed anyone from out of the house?"

"Well." I hesitate. "Not yet. Not exactly."

Dr. Sarah waits. This is what she does, like a cop waiting to catch out a criminal. And every time I say I won't crack first, but I always do.

"OK, there's this boy, Linus," I hear myself saying.

"Yes, you've mentioned him." She nods.

"He used to come round to see Frank and I was going to interview him. Only now he doesn't come round anymore. So I thought . . . I mean . . ."

I trail off, not sure what I do mean.

"Maybe you should ask him," says Dr. Sarah, like it's no big deal.

"I can't," I say automatically.

"Why not?"

"Because . . ." I lapse into silence. She knows why not. It doesn't need saying.

"Let's visualize the worst that can happen," says Dr. Sarah cheerfully. "You ask Linus to come over and he says no. How does that make you feel?"

Trickles of anxiety are running down my back. I don't like this conversation anymore. I should never have mentioned Linus.

"How does that make you feel?" persists Dr. Sarah. "Audrey, work with me. Linus has just said, 'No, I won't come over.' What are you feeling?"

"I'm totally embarrassed," I say miserably. "I'm dying. I'm like, oh my God. Like, I'm so *stupid* . . . " I screw up my face in agony.

"Why stupid?"

"Because— *Because!*" I look at her almost angrily. Sometimes Dr. Sarah is deliberately obtuse.

"Linus won't come over." She gets up and writes it on the board:

Linus won't come over.

Then she draws an arrow from it and writes *Linus's thoughts* in a circle.

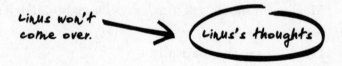

"Why should these thoughts"—she taps the board—"make you feel stupid?"

"Because . . ." I struggle with my own thought process. "Because I shouldn't have asked him."

"Why not?" she counters. "So he says no. All that means is, he didn't feel like being interviewed, or he was busy, or he's intending to say yes another time. Or any number of things. It doesn't mean anything about you."

"Of course it does!" I say before I can stop myself.

"Of course?" She instantly picks me up on it. *"Of course?"*

OK, I fell into that one. *Of course* is the kind of phrase that makes Dr. Sarah's nose twitch like a shark scenting blood. That and *I have to.*

"Audrey, do you know what Linus is thinking?"

"No," I say reluctantly.

"You don't sound sure about that. Audrey, can you see into people's heads?"

"No."

"Are you gifted with superpowers? Is this something I should know about you?"

"No." I hold up my hands. "OK. I get it. I was mind-reading."

"You were mind-reading." She nods. "You have no idea what Linus is thinking. It could be good, it could be bad. Most likely, it's nothing at all. He's a boy. You'd better get used to that." Her face crinkles in humour.

"Right." I know she's trying to make me smile, but I'm too confused. "So . . . I should ask him?"

"I think you should." She picks up the whiteboard cloth and rubs out *Linus won't come over.* In its place, she writes:

Linus might come over.
He might not. Either way
is fine. Either way, his   ──────➤ ⬭Linus's thoughts⬭
decision is about himself,
not about you. You are
    not responsible for
        his feelings.

"OK?" she says, when I've had a chance to read it.

"OK."

"Good. Then ask him. Let's make that your homework. Asking Linus."

The first step is catching Mum in a good mood, when she's not going to freak out or overreact or anything. I wait till she's just finished watching an episode of *MasterChef*, then casually sit on the arm of the sofa and say,

"Mum, I'd like a phone."

"A phone?" She sits up, her eyes wide circles, her mouth open. "A *phone*?"

If I'm the Queen of Overreaction, Mum is the Empress.

"Um, yes. A phone. If that's OK."

"Who are you going to call?" she demands.

"I just . . . I don't know. People." I know I sound scratchy, but she makes me scratchy.

"Which people?"

"People! Do you, like, need all their names?"

There's silence, and I know what she's thinking, because I'm thinking it too. My last phone wasn't exactly a success. I mean, it was a nice phone. It was a Samsung. But it became like this portal. A kind of toxic portal to . . . all of it. It used to make me quiver with fright, just hearing the buzz of a text, let alone reading it. I don't know what happened to it. Dad got rid of it.

But I mean, that was then.

That was them.

"Audrey . . ." Mum's face is strained and I feel sorry I've ruined her nice evening of *MasterChef* and *Grand Designs* or whatever.

"It'll be fine," I reassure her.

"Do you want to call Natalie? Is that it?"

The name *Natalie* makes me shrink away a little. I'm not sure I'm quite ready to talk to Natalie. But nor do I want to give anything away to Mum.

"Maybe." I shrug.

"Audrey, I don't know . . ."

I know why Mum's sensitive on this issue. I mean believe me, I'm sensitive too. (In fact, I'm *over*sensitive, which basically the whole world has told me.) But I'm not giving in. I feel resolved on this. I should get a phone.

"Audrey, be careful. I just . . . I just don't want you to be . . ."

"I know."

I can see a few grey hairs among Mum's vivid brown highlights. Her skin looks kind of thin. I think all this has aged her. *I've* aged her.

"Dr. Sarah would tell me to get the phone," I say, to make her feel better. "She always says I can text her, any time. She says I'll know when I'm ready. Well, I'm ready."

"OK." Mum sighs. "We'll get you a phone. I mean, it's great that you want one, darling. It's wonderful." She puts a hand on mine as though she's only just seeing the positive side. "This is progress!"

"I haven't used it yet," I remind her. "Don't get too excited." I sit properly on the sofa and shift up a bit. "What are you watching?"

As I'm moving the cushions around, I see a book, nestled in Mum's lap. It's entitled *How to Talk to Your Teens* by Dr. Terence Kirshenberger.

"Oh my *God*." I pick it up. "Mum, what is this?"

Mum flushes pink and grabs it.

"Nothing. Just some reading matter."

"You don't need a *book* to talk to us!" I flip through the pages and see lots of lame-looking cartoons, then turn to the back. "Twelve ninety-five? You spent twelve ninety-five on this? What does it say? I bet it says, 'Your teenager is a person too.'"

"No, it says, 'Give me my book back.'" Mum grabs the book before I can stop her and sits on it. "OK, now are we watching TV?"

She's still pink, though, and looks kind of embarrassed. Poor Mum. I can't believe she spent £12.95 on a book full of crap cartoons.

◆ ◆ ◆

She read it! She read the £12.95 book!

The reason I know is that on Saturday she suddenly starts talking to Frank at breakfast like she's speaking a foreign language.

"So, Frank, I noticed you left two wet towels on the floor of your bedroom yesterday," she begins, in weird, calm tones. "That made me feel surprised. How did it make you feel?"

"Huh?" Frank stares at her.

"I think we could find a solution to the towel issue together," Mum continues. "I think that could be a fun challenge."

Frank looks at me, baffled, and I shrug.

"What do you think, Frank?" persists Mum. "If you were running this house, what would you advise about towels?"

"Dunno." Frank looks a bit unnerved. "Use kitchen towel and chuck it away."

I can tell Mum is a bit frustrated with that answer, but she keeps on smiling this weird smile.

"I hear you," she says. "Interesting idea."

"It's not." Frank looks at her suspiciously.

"Yes it is."

"Mum, it's a stupid idea I invented to piss you off. You can't say 'It's interesting.'"

"I hear you." Mum nods. "I hear you, Frank. I can see your point of view. It's valid."

"I don't have a point of view!" Frank snaps. "And stop saying 'I hear you.'"

"Mum read a book," I tell him. "It's called *How to Talk to Your Teens.*"

"Oh for fuck's sake." Frank rolls his eyes.

"Do *not* swear, young man!" Mum snaps straight out of her Stepford Mum mode.

"Oh, for futtsake!" chimes in Felix joyfully, and Mum inhales furiously.

"You see? You see what you did?"

"Well, stop talking to me like a bloody robot!" shouts Frank. "It's totally fake."

"Bloody robot!" echoes Felix.

"That book cost twelve ninety-five," I tell Frank, who gives an incredulous laugh.

"Twelve ninety-five! I could write that book in four words. It would say 'Stop patronizing your teenager.'"

There's silence. I think Mum's making an effort not to lose it. From the way she's crushing her napkin into a tiny ball, I think she's finding it quite hard. At last she looks up with a smile again.

"Frank, I understand you're frustrated with life at the moment," she says, in pleasant tones. "So I've found you some occupations. You can do some jamming with Dad today and next week you're volunteering."

"Volunteering?" Frank looks taken aback. "Like, building huts in Africa?"

"Making sandwiches for the Avonlea fete."

Avonlea is the old people's home in the next street. They have this fete every year and it's quite fun. You know. For a thing in a garden with old people.

"Making *sandwiches*?" Frank looks aghast. "You're joking."

"I've volunteered our kitchen for the catering. We're all going to help."

"I'm not making bloody sandwiches."

"I hear you," says Mum. "But you are. And don't swear."

"I'm not."

"I hear you, Frank," says Mum implacably. "But you are."

"Mum stop it, OK?"

"I hear you."

"*Stop* it."

"I hear you."

"Stop it! Jesus!" Frank brings two fists to his head. "OK, I'll make the bloody sandwiches! Now have you finished ruining my life?"

He swings away from the table and Mum gives a tiny smile.

INTERIOR. 5 ROSEWOOD CLOSE. DAY.

The camera approaches the garage doors. Inside we find
Dad dressed in leathers, holding a guitar connected
to a massive amp. Frank is standing nearby, holding a
bass, looking dismal.

> **DAD**
> (enthusiastically)
> So let's jam. Just play around, have
> some fun.

He plays a showy guitar riff.

> **DAD**
> You know "For Her, For Me"?

> **FRANK**
> What?

> **DAD**
> "For Her, For Me." It's our best-known
> song.

He looks a little hurt.

> **DAD**
> I sent you the link? I have a solo on
> that track.

He plays another showy guitar riff.

> **FRANK**
> Right. Er . . . I don't know it.

> **DAD**
> What do you know?

                         FRANK
          I know the theme tune to *LOC*.

He starts to play it, but Dad shakes his head
impatiently.

                          DAD
          We want to play *real* music. OK, we'll
          just jam over the chord structure. Keep
          it simple. Intro—C E, F, G, chorus
          in double time—D minor, F, C for two
          beats, chorus repeats with a G chord
          for a pickup to go into the verse.

Frank stares at him in panic.

                         FRANK
          What?

                          DAD
          Just feel it. You'll be fine. A one, a
          two, a one-two-three-four.

A cacophony of music hits the air as both start
playing. Dad starts singing in a screechy voice.

                          DAD
                    (sings)
          For her . . . for meeeeee . . . Comin'
          round again . . .
                    (shouts above music)
          You do backing, Frank.
                    (sings)
          For her, for meeeee . . .

He launches into a solo. Frank stares wildly at the
camera and mouths "Help."

INTERIOR. 5 ROSEWOOD CLOSE. DAY.

Mum is making lunch in the kitchen as Dad enters, all fired up. She looks up.

> **MUM**
> So? How was that?

> **DAD**
> It was great! We jammed, we bonded . . .
> I think Frank really enjoyed it.

> **MUM**
> Great! Well done!

She gives him a hug.

MY SERENE AND LOVING FAMILY—FILM TRANSCRIPT

INTERIOR. 5 ROSEWOOD CLOSE. DAY.

Frank sits at the top of the stairs. He addresses the
camera.

> **FRANK**
> Oh my God. That was the single worst
> experience of my life.

> **AUDREY (VOICE-OVER)**
> No it wasn't.

> **FRANK**
> (scowls)
> You don't know. Maybe it was.

He sags against the bannister.

> **FRANK**
> Why does Dad want to play old-man rock
> with me? Why?

> **AUDREY (V.O.)**
> To stop you playing computer games.

Frank gives her a dark look.

> **FRANK**
> Thanks, Einstein.

> **AUDREY (V.O.)**
> I'm just telling you. They want you to
> have other interests.

> **FRANK**
> (explodes)
> I don't want any other interests! What's
> wrong with gaming?

                    AUDREY (V.O.)
I didn't say anything was wrong with gaming.

                        FRANK
Gaming develops your reaction times, it
helps teamwork and strategy, it teaches
you stuff . . .

                    AUDREY (V.O.)
                    (sceptically)
It teaches you stuff? What stuff?

                        FRANK
OK, you want to know? (He counts off on
his fingers.) *Minecraft*—architecture.
SimCity—how to manage a population and
budget and shit. *Assassin's Creed*—ancient
Rome and the Borgias and like . . .
Leonardo da Vinci. Everything. All the
history I remember comes from *Assassin's
Creed*. None from school. All from gaming.

                    AUDREY (V.O.)
What have you learned from *LOC*?

                        FRANK
                        (grins)
Mostly Korean curse words. (He suddenly
shouts.) SHEEBSEKEE!

                    AUDREY (V.O.)
What does that mean?

                        FRANK
Use your imagination.

From downstairs, Mum calls.

                           MUM
          Frank! Audrey! Lunchtime!

Frank doesn't even seem to hear.

                          FRANK
          You know in lots of countries *LOC* is
          a spectator sport? You know they have
          arenas?

                       AUDREY (V.O.)
          I know. You told me like a million
          times.

                          FRANK
          You know in the States they have *LOC*
          scholarships at some universities?

                       AUDREY (V.O.)
          You told me that too.

                          FRANK
          LOC is sophisticated. It has its own
          language. It has rules. It's like . . .
          it's like fucking *Latin*. That's what
          it's like. Latin. And Mum and Dad are
          like, "Oh it's so evil." What if I was
          addicted to Latin?

A long pause.

                       AUDREY (V.O.)
          I honestly can't imagine that.

So Mum's bought me a phone. That was step one. I've got Linus's number off Frank. That was step two. Now I need to call him.

I input his number and stare at it for a while. I try to imagine how I'll start the conversation. I write down some useful words and phrases I might need. (Dr. Sarah's tip.) I visualize a positive scenario.

But I still can't bring myself to call him. So instead I text.

> Hi, Linus. This is Audrey here. Frank's sister. I still need to do my documentary and you said you would be interviewed for it. Is that still OK? Could we meet? Thanks, Audrey.

And I'm expecting no reply, or at least a long wait, but the phone buzzes straight away and there's his response:

> Sure. When?

I hadn't thought about that. When? It's Saturday evening, which means we've got all day tomorrow.

Tomorrow? Do you want to come round here? 11 a.m.?

I press Send, and this time there's a bit of a wait before he replies:

No, let's meet at Starbucks.

A jolt of panic goes through me like white fire. Starbucks? Is he nuts? Then a second text comes through:

You have to go there anyway, right? Isn't that your project?

But . . . but . . . but . . .
Starbucks?
Tomorrow?
My fingers are trembling. My skin feels hot. I'm breathing in for four counts and out for seven and trying to channel Dr. Sarah. How would she advise me? What would she say?
But already I know what she'd say. Because she's said it. I can hear her voice in my head, right now:
It's time for some bigger steps.
You need to push yourself, Audrey.
You won't know till you try.
I believe you can cope with it.
I stare at the phone till the numbers blur in front of my eyes, then type the text before I can change my mind.

OK. See you there.

I know what it's like to be an old person now.

OK, I don't know what it's like to have wrinkly skin and white hair. But I *do* know what it's like to walk down the road at a slow, uncertain pace, wincing at the passing of people, and flinching when horns beep and feeling like everything is just too *fast*.

Mum and Dad have taken Felix out for the day to some garden show, and at the last minute they took Frank too to "broaden his horizons." So they have no idea I'm doing this. I couldn't face the whole big deal of telling them and Mum fussing and all that palaver. So I waited till they left, got my key, got my money and the camera, and just left the house.

Which I haven't done for . . .

I don't know. *So* long.

We live about twenty minutes' walk from Starbucks, if

you're striding. I'm not striding. But I'm not stopping either. I'm going. Even though my lizard brain is poised to curl up in fright, I'm managing to put one foot in front of the other. Left, right. Left, right.

My dark glasses are on, my hands are jammed in the pockets of my hoodie, and I've pulled the hood up for extra protection. I haven't raised my gaze from the pavement but that's OK. Most people walk along in their own worlds anyway.

As I reach the town centre the crowds become denser and the shop fronts are bright and noisy and with every step I have a stronger desire to run, but I don't. I push on. It's like climbing a mountain, I tell myself. Your body doesn't want to do it, but you make it.

And then, at last, I've made it to Starbucks. As I approach the familiar façade I feel kind of exhausted, but I'm giddy too. I'm here. I'm here!

I push the door open and there's Linus, sitting at a table near the entrance. He's wearing jeans and a grey T-shirt and he looks hot, I notice before I can stop myself. Not that this is a date.

I mean, *obviously* it's not a date. But even so—

Midsentence Stop. Whatever. You know what I mean.

Linus's face brightens as he sees me, and he leaps up from the table.

"You made it!"

"Yes!"

"I didn't think you would."

"I didn't think so either," I admit.

"But you did! You're cured!"

His enthusiasm is so infectious I grin madly back and we sort of do a mini-dance, arms waving up and down.

"Shall we get some coffee?"

"Yes!" I say, in my new confident, everything's-fine way. "Great!"

As we join the queue I feel kind of wired. The music on the sound system is too loud and the conversations around me are hitting my eardrums with a force that makes me wince, but I'm going with it instead of resisting. Like you do at a rock concert, when your nerves get taken over by the force of the noise and you just have to surrender. (And yes, I appreciate most people would not equate low-level Starbucks chatter to a rock concert. All I will say is: Try living inside my brain for a bit.)

I can feel my heart pumping, but whether it's because of the noise or the people or because I'm with a hot-looking boy, I don't know. I give my order (caramel Frappuccino) and the surly girl behind the counter says, "Name?"

If there's one thing I don't want it's my name being shouted across a busy coffee shop.

"I hate the name thing," I mutter to Linus.

"Me too." He nods. "Give a fake one. I always do."

"Name?" repeats the girl impatiently.

"Oh. Um, Rhubarb," I say.

"Rhubarb?"

It's easy to keep a poker face when you're wearing dark glasses and a hoodie and you're looking off to one side.

"Yes, that's my name. Rhubarb."

"You're called *Rhubarb*?"

"Of course she's called Rhubarb," chimes in Linus.

"Hey, Rhu, do you want anything to eat? You want a muffin, Rhu?"

"No, thanks." I can't help smiling.

"OK, Rhu. No problem."

"Fine. Rhu-barb." The girl writes it down with her Sharpie. "And you?"

"I would like a cappuccino," says Linus politely. "Thank you."

"Your name?"

"I'll spell it for you," he says. "Z-W-P-A-E-N—"

"What?" She stares at him, Sharpie in hand

"Wait. I haven't finished. Double-F-hyphen-T-J-U-S. It's an unusual name," Linus adds gravely. "It's Dutch."

I'm shaking, trying not to laugh. The Starbucks girl gives us both evil stares.

"You're John," she says, and scrawls it on his cup.

I tell Linus I'll pay because this is my documentary and I'm the producer, and he says OK, he'll get the next one. Then we take our cups—Rhubarb and John—and head back to our table. My heart is pounding even harder, but I'm on a high. Look at me! In Starbucks! Back to normal!

I mean, OK, I'm still in dark glasses. And I can't look at anyone. And my hands are doing weird twisty things in my lap. But I'm here. That's the point.

"So you dumped Frank off your team," I say as we sit down, and immediately regret it in case it sounds aggressive.

But Linus doesn't look offended. He looks worried. "Frank doesn't blame me," he says quickly, and I realize they must have had a conversation about this. "I mean, he wouldn't expect us all to give up playing *LOC* just because he's had to. He said he'd do the same if it was him."

"So who's the fourth?"

"This guy Matt," says Linus without enthusiasm. "He's OK."

"Dad made Frank play bass with him in the garage," I tell him. "He thinks that's a better interest."

"Does Frank play bass?"

"Barely." I snuffle with laughter. "He plays, like, three chords and Dad does ten-minute solos."

"You think that's bad? My dad plays the recorder."

"He *what*?" My laughter dies away. "Seriously?"

"You can't tell anyone." Linus looks suddenly vulnerable and I feel a wave of . . . something. Something strong and warm. Like when you put your arm round someone and squeeze.

"I won't tell. I promise." I take a sip of Frappuccino. "Like, the kind of recorder kids play?"

"A grown-up kind. Wooden. Big." He demonstrates.

"Wow. I didn't know that existed."

We sip our drinks and smile at each other. Thoughts are racing through my head, crazy thoughts like *I've made it! I'm in Starbucks! Go me!* But there are other, weird, random thoughts popping up, like *Everyone's looking at me* and *I hate myself.* And then suddenly *I wish I was at home right now,* which is just weird. I do *not* wish I was at home. I'm out with Linus! In Starbucks!

"So what do you want to ask me on your documentary?" he says.

"Oh, I don't know. Stuff."

"Is this part of your therapy?"

"Yes. Kind of."

"But do you still need therapy? I mean, you look fine."

"Well, I am fine. It's just this project . . ."

"If you just took off your dark glasses you'd be, like, totally back to normal. You should do that," Linus says with enthusiasm. "You know, just *do* it."

"I will."

"But you shouldn't wait. You should do it, right here, right now."

"Yes. Maybe."

"Shall I do it?" He reaches over and I recoil.

My bravado is melting away. His voice feels hectoring, like he's giving me an interrogation.

I don't know what's happened in my head. Things have turned. I take a sip of Frappuccino, trying to relax, but all I really want to do is grab a napkin and shred it into little bits. The voices around me are getting louder and louder; more and more threatening.

At the counter, someone's complaining about a cold coffee, and I find myself tuning in to the only side of the argument that I can hear.

"Complained three times— Don't want a free coffee— Not good enough! Just not good enough!"

The angry voice is like a chisel in my brain. It's making me flinch and close my eyes and want to flee. I'm starting to panic. My chest is rising and falling. I can't stay. I can't do this. Dr. Sarah's wrong. I'm never going to get better. Look, I can't even sit in Starbucks. I'm a total failure.

And now darker thoughts are circling my head, dragging me down. *I should just hide away. I shouldn't even exist. What's the point of me, anyway?*

"Audrey?" Linus waves a hand in front of my face, which makes me flinch even more. "Audrey?"

"I'm sorry," I gulp, and push my chair back. I have to escape.

"What?" Linus stares at me, bewildered.

"I can't stay."

"Why?"

"It's just . . . too loud. Too much." I put my hands over my ears. "Sorry. I'm so sorry . . ."

I'm already at the door. I push it open and feel some small relief as I make it outside. But I'm not safe. I'm not home.

"But you were fine." Linus has followed me out. He sounds almost angry. "You were fine just now! We were chatting and we were laughing . . ."

"I know."

"So what happened?"

"Nothing," I say desperately. "I don't know. It makes no sense."

"So, just tell yourself to snap out of it. You know, mind over matter."

"I've tried!" Angry tears rise in my eyes. "Don't you think I've *tried* snapping out of it?"

My head is a whirling mass of distress signals. I have to go. Now. I never hail taxis, ever, but right now I don't even think twice. I stick my hand out and a black cab comes trundling by. Tears are filling my eyes as I get in—not that anyone can see them.

"Sorry," I say to Linus, my voice a little thick. "I really am. So. We should forget the film and everything. So. I won't see you, I guess. Bye. Sorry. Sorry."

◆ ◆ ◆

At home I lie in my bed, totally still, totally silent, with the curtains drawn and earplugs in. For about three hours. I don't move a muscle. Sometimes I feel as if I'm a phone, and this is the only way I can recharge. Dr. Sarah says my body is on an adrenaline roller coaster, and that's why I lurch from totally wired to totally fatigued, with nothing in between.

At last, feeling wobbly, I head downstairs for something to eat. I write a text to Dr. Sarah:

I went to Starbucks but I had a meltdown,

and send it off. The dark, ill thoughts have gone, but they've left me feeling weak and jittery.

I drift into the kitchen, and wince as I pass my reflection in the mirror. I look pale and kind of . . . I don't know. Shrunken. It's like the flu. It attacks you and your whole body takes the hit. I'm just considering whether to make a Nutella sandwich or a cheese one when I hear a rattling sound from the hall, and something dropping on the mat, and I jump a mile.

For a moment there's silence. I've tensed up all over like an animal in a trap, but I tell myself firmly, *I am safe, I am safe, I am safe,* and my heart rate slowly drops, and at last I wander out to see what it is.

It's a note, on the doormat—a piece of lined paper torn out of a notebook with *Audrey* written in Linus's handwriting. I open it to see:

Are you OK? I texted but you didn't reply. Frank didn't reply either. I didn't want to ring the doorbell and shock you. Are you OK??

I haven't even looked at my phone since I texted Dr. Sarah. And Frank's at the garden show, in the countryside. He probably hasn't got any signal. I imagine Frank, grimly tramping round some field, and raise a faint smile. He'll be in *such* a bad mood.

Through the ripply glass of the front door I suddenly notice a kind of shadowy movement, and my heart catches. Oh God. Is that Linus, there? Is he waiting? For what?

I reach for a pen and think for a moment.

I'm fine, thank you, sorry I freaked out.

I push it back through the letter box. It's a bit difficult because there's a spring, but I manage it. A moment later, it reappears.

You looked really bad. I was worried.

I stare at his words, my heart falling like a stone. *Really bad.* I looked *really bad.* I ruin everything.

Sorry.

Somehow I can't find anything to put except that one word, so I write it again.

Sorry. Sorry.

And I post the letter back through the letter box. Almost at once the page is pushed back with his reply:

No, don't be sorry. It's not your fault. In Starbucks, what were you thinking?

I wasn't expecting that. For a few moments I don't move. I'm hunched on the doormat, thoughts running through my head like ticker tape. Do I answer? What do I answer?

Do I want to tell him what I was thinking?

The voice of that therapist from St. John's keeps running through my head; the one who used to take the Self-Assertion workshop. *We do not have to reveal ourselves.* She used to say it every week. *We are all entitled to privacy. You do not have to share anything with others, however much they may ask you. Photos, fantasies, plans for the weekend . . . they're yours.* She used to look around the room almost sternly. *You do NOT have to share them.*

I don't have to share with Linus what I was thinking. I could walk away. I could write, *Oh, nothing!* Or, *You don't want to know!!! ;)* Like it's all a big joke.

But somehow . . . I want to share. I don't know why, but I do. I trust him. And he's on the other side of the door. It's all safe. Like in a confessional.

Before I can change my mind, I scrawl,

I was thinking, "I'm a total failure, I shouldn't exist, what's the point of me?"

I shove it through the letter box, sit back on my heels, and blow out, feeling a strange satisfaction. There. Enough pretending. Now he knows just how weird the inside of my mind is. I hold my breath, trying to glean his reaction on the other side of the door, but there's silence. The ripply glass is still. I can't detect any response at all. I think he must have gone. Of course he's gone. Who would stay?

Oh God, am I *nuts*? Why would I write down my most warped thoughts and post them through a letter box to the one guy I actually like? Why would I do this?

Totally deflated, I get to my feet, and I've reached the kitchen door when I hear a rattling. I whip round—and there's a reply on the doormat. My hands are trembling as I grab it, and at first I can't focus properly. It's a new page, covered in writing, and it begins,

What's the point of you? Try this, for starters.

And underneath there's a long list. He's written a long, long list, that fills the page. I'm so flustered, I can't even read it properly, but as I scan down I catch *beautiful smile* and *great taste in music (I sneaked a look at your iPod)* and *awesome Starbucks name.*

I give a sudden snort of laughter that almost turns to a sob and then turns to a smile, and then suddenly I'm wiping my eyes. I'm all over the place.

With a rattle, another note plops through the letter box and I jerk in shock. What more can he have to say? Not another great big list, surely? But it says:

Will you open the door?

A flurry of alarm races through me. I can't let him see my shrunken, pale, ratty self. I just can't. I know Dr. Sarah would tell me I'm not shrunken or ratty, I'm imagining it, but she's not here, is she?

Not quite up to it. Another time. Sorry, sorry ...

I hold my breath after I've posted the page. He'll be offended. He'll leave. That's it, all over, before it even began ...

But then the letter box rattles yet again and a reply comes through:

Understood. I'll be off, then.

My spirits plunge. He *is* leaving. He *is* offended. He hates me, I should have opened the door, I should have been stronger, I'm so stupid ... I'm just trying desperately to think of what I can write, when another page drops onto the mat. It's folded over, and on the outside is written:

Had to give you this before I go.

For a few moments I don't dare read it. But at last I open it up and stare at the words inside. My head is prickling all over with disbelief. My breath is jumpy as I read it. He wrote that. He wrote that. To me.

It's a kiss.

At St. John's, they tell you not to keep rewinding your thoughts and going over old ground. They tell you to live in the present, not the past. But how are you supposed to do that when a boy you like has just kind of, virtually, kissed you?

By the time I see Dr. Sarah at my next session I've replayed the scene like a million times, and now I'm wondering if the whole thing was just him winding me up, or having something to laugh about with his friends, or was he just being polite? I mean, does he feel sorry for me? Was it a pity kiss? Oh God. It was so a pity kiss. (Not that I'm an expert on kisses. I have kissed precisely one boy in my life, which was on holiday last year and it was gross.)

Dr. Sarah listens politely for about half an hour as I blabber on about Linus. And then we talk about "mind-reading" and "catastrophising," just like I knew we would. I think I could be a therapist myself, sometimes.

"I know what you'll tell me," I say at last. "I can't read his mind and I shouldn't try. But how can I not think about it? He *kissed* me. I mean . . . sort of. On paper." I shrug, feeling a bit embarrassed. "You probably think it doesn't count."

"Not at all," says Dr. Sarah seriously. "The fact that it was on paper doesn't lessen it. A kiss is a kiss."

"And now I haven't heard from him and I have no idea what he's thinking, and it stresses me out . . ." Dr. Sarah doesn't reply immediately, and I sigh. "I know, I know. I have an illness and it's fully treatable."

There's another long silence. Dr. Sarah's mouth is twitching.

"You know, Audrey?" she says at last. "I hate to break it to you, but getting stressed over what boys are thinking after they've kissed you may not be fully treatable. Not *fully.*"

◆ ◆ ◆

And then, three days after Starbucks, I'm sitting watching TV peacefully on my own when Frank comes stomping into the den and says, "Linus is here."

"Oh, right." I sit up in a fluster. "Really? He's here? But . . ." I swallow. "You're not allowed to play *LOC*, so . . . I mean, why is he . . ."

"He wants to see *you*." Frank sounds fairly unimpressed by this fact. "Is that OK? You won't freak out?"

"No. Yes. I mean . . . that's fine."

"Good, because he's here. Lin-*us*!"

Some brothers would give their sister a chance to brush their hair. Or at least change out of the scaggy old T-shirt they've been in all day. I'm sending murderous thought waves to Frank as Linus comes into the den and says cautiously, "Hi. Wow, it's dark in here."

Everyone in the family has got so used to my darkened den, I forget how it must look to other people. I keep the blackout curtains closed and the lights off, and the only illumination is the flickering telly. And then I feel safe. Safe enough to take my dark glasses off.

"Yes. Sorry."

"No, it's fine. You really are rhubarb."

"That's my name." I see him smile through the darkness. There's a glow on his teeth from the TV, and his eyes are two shining chinks.

I'm sitting in my customary place on the carpet and after a moment he comes over and sits down next to me. I mean, not *right* next to me. He's about a foot away. I think my skin must be able to send out signals like a bat, because I'm totally aware of his position in relation to mine. And all the time my head is buzzing with the thought: *He kissed me. On paper. Kind of. He kissed me.*

"What are you watching?" He stares at the telly, where a woman in a tailored dress is trying to find things to say about kelp shampoo. "Is that QVC?"

"Yes. I find the conversations soothing."

QVC is the most calming TV I know. You have three people in a studio and they all think the moisturiser is great. No-one argues the point or raises their voice. No-one discovers they're pregnant or gets murdered. And there's no studio laughter, which believe me, can sound like a drill in my head.

"Don't worry, I know I'm nuts," I add.

"You think this is nuts?" says Linus. "You want to meet my granny. She's *really* nuts. She thinks she's twenty-five. When she looks in the mirror she thinks we're playing tricks on her. She can't see reality. She wears miniskirts, she wants to go out to dances . . . She wears more makeup than any granny you've ever seen."

"She sounds awesome!"

"She's . . . you know." He shrugs. "Sometimes it's funny, sometimes it's sad. But the point is, she's not twenty-five, is she? It's just her sick brain telling her that, isn't it?"

He seems to expect an answer, so I say, "Right."

"I meant to say this to you, before. After Starbucks. Do you get what I'm saying?" He sounds emphatic. "Gran's not twenty-five, and you're not . . . whatever all that bad stuff in your head was telling you. You're *not* that."

And suddenly I see what he's doing, what he's trying to do.

"Right," I say again. "Yes. I know."

And I do know. Although it's easier to know when the bad thoughts aren't rushing through your head like a river.

"Thanks," I add. "Thanks for . . . you know. Understanding. Getting it."

"I don't really get it. But . . ."

"You do, more than most people. Really."

"Well." He sounds awkward. "Anyway. So, are you feeling better now?"

"Loads better." I smile in his direction. "Loads and loads better."

The ladies on QVC have moved onto a vegetable chopper,

and for a while we watch it demolishing carrots and cabbages. Then Linus says,

"How's the shoe contact coming along?"

At the word *contact* I stiffen inside. *Contact.* Not just on paper, for real.

Don't think I haven't thought about it.

"Haven't tried it again." I'm trying hard to sound casual.

"Do you want to?"

"OK."

I shift my shoe over till it's touching his. Shoe to shoe, like we did before. I'm poised for a meltdown, for a freak-out, for some totally embarrassing reaction. But the strange thing is ... it doesn't happen. My body hasn't squirmed away. My breathing is even. My lizard brain is, like, all Zen and relaxed. What's going on?

"It's the darkness," I say out loud, before I can stop myself. "It's the *darkness*." I feel almost heady with relief.

"What is?"

"I can relax when it's dark. It's like, the world is a different place." I spread my arms out in the dark, feeling it against my skin like a soft, enveloping cushion. "I think I could do anything if the whole world was dark the whole time. You know. I'd be fine."

"Then you should be a potholer," suggests Linus. "Or a caver."

"Or a bat."

"A vampire."

"Oh my God, I should *so* be a vampire."

"Except the whole eating people thing."

"Yerk." I nod, agreeing.

"Doesn't it get monotonous? People's blood every night? Don't they ever want a plate of chips?"

"I don't know." I feel a giggle rise. "Next time I see a vampire I'll ask him."

We watch the vegetable chopper make way for a steam cooker which has sold 145 units already, this hour.

"So, bearing in mind it's dark and all," says Linus, casually, "what about . . . thumb contact? Just to see if you can do it. Like an experiment."

"Right." I nod, feeling a little flip in my stomach. "Um. OK. Why not?"

I feel his hand make its way towards mine. Our thumbs find each other and his skin is dry and warm and kind of how I expected it to be. His thumbnail circles mine and I playfully dodge his, and he laughs.

"So you're OK with thumb contact."

"Thumb contact is good." I nod.

He doesn't say anything more, but I can feel him extending his thumb down into the palm of my hand. We're into finger-to-hand contact. And then palm-to-palm contact. His hand clasps mine and I squeeze back.

Now he's shifting closer and with more intent. I can feel the warmth of him, through the air, against my arm, against my leg. And now I'm a little keyed up, but not like I was in Starbucks. There's nothing crazy running through my head. In fact, I'm not sure anything's running through my head at all except *Is this happening for real?* And *Yes it is.*

"Jeans contact OK?" he murmurs, as his leg twines round mine.

"Yes, jeans contact is good," I manage.

We've reached arm-round-shoulders contact. Hair-to-hair contact. Cheek-to-cheek contact. His face feels gently rough as he slides it along mine.

Mouth contact.

He doesn't say anything about it or ask if it's OK. I don't say anything either. But it is OK. It's more than OK.

When we've kissed, like, forever, he shuffles up and sits me on his knee, and I curl into him. He feels warm and solid. His arms feel strong around me. And his hair smells nice. And it's pretty hard to concentrate on the benefits of a food processor with four unique attachments, on special exclusive offer today for only £69.99.

◆ ◆ ◆

Here's the really embarrassing thing: I fell asleep. I don't know if it was a post-adrenaline crash or just the Clonazepam I'd taken at lunchtime—but I did. When I woke, I was spread-eagled on the floor and Mum was calling me from the hall, and the ladies on QVC were talking about a magic chip fryer that halves the calories. And next to me there was a note.

I'll see you soon. XXX

I've gone up a level. That's the only way I can describe it.

If I was a hero in *LOC* I'd have like enhanced attributes, or some extra kick-ass weapon or something. I'm stronger. I feel taller. I bounce back quicker. It's been a week since Linus and I watched QVC and yes, I've had one bad episode, but I didn't sink quite as low. Things weren't quite as dark.

Linus has come over a few times and we always watch QVC and just chat or whatever and it's just . . . Well. It's good. Now it's Friday afternoon and even though I'm not at school, I've got that end-of-week feeling. The air's warm and I can hear children playing in their gardens. From the kitchen window I watch Felix running round the lawn with no clothes on and a watering can in his fist.

I hear the tinkle of an ice-cream van and I'm about to call out to Mum that we should get Felix an ice lolly, when she comes into the kitchen. Staggers, more like. Her face is so pale it's like *mauve*. And she actually holds on to the kitchen island as though otherwise she might fall over.

"Mum?" I eye her in alarm. "Are you OK?" At once I realize this is a stupid question. She's not OK, she's poorly. "I think you should go to bed."

"I'm fine." She gives me a weak smile.

"You're not! You've got a bug. You need rest and fluids. Have you got a temperature?" I'm trying to remember all the things she says to us when we're ill. "Would you like a Lemsip?"

"Oh, a Lemsip." She breathes out, looking like a wraith. "Yes, that would be nice."

"I'll look after Felix," I say firmly. "You go to bed. I'll bring the Lemsip up."

I flip on the kettle and am rooting around in the cupboards for the Lemsip packet, when Frank arrives home. I can tell this from the almighty crash that comes from the hall. That'll be his school bag, a sports bag, his cricket bat, and whatever other junk he's got, all being dumped from a great height onto the tiles. He comes into the kitchen, singing some tuneless song and peeling off his tie.

"All right!" He punches the air, singing, "It's the weeeeeek-end . . . What's for supper?"

"Mum's ill," I tell him. "She's got, like, flu or something. I told her to go to bed. You should go out and buy her . . ." I think for a moment. "Grapes."

"I've only just got home." Frank looks unenthusiastic. "And I'm starving."

"Well, have a sandwich and *then* get her some grapes."

"What good do grapes do?"

"Dunno," I say impatiently. "It's what you have when you're ill."

I've made the Lemsip and found a couple of biscuits, and I put them all on a tray.

"Get Ribena too." I say. "And whatsit. Nurofen. Write it down." I turn to make sure Frank is listening—but he's not writing anything down. He's just standing there, giving me this weird, very un-Frank look. His head is tilted and he looks sort of fascinated, or curious, or *something*. "What?" I say defensively. "Look, I know it's Friday, but Mum's ill."

"I know," says Frank. "It's not that. It's . . ." He hesitates. "D'you know something, Aud? You wouldn't have done this when you first came back from hospital. You've changed."

I'm so taken aback, I don't know what to say. Like, first of all, I didn't think Frank ever noticed things about me. And second of all, is that true? I try to think back, but it's a bit hazy. This is a side-effect of depression, Dr. Sarah has told me. Your memory gets shot to pieces. Which, you know, can be a good thing or a bad thing.

"Really?" I say at last.

"You would have just hidden in your room. Everything got you into a state, even the doorbell ringing. But now look. You're in charge. You're on top of it." He nods at me holding the tray. "It's . . . well . . . It's good. It's cool."

"Thanks," I say awkwardly.

"No probs." He looks equally awkward. Then he opens the fridge, gets out a carton of chocolate milk and plugs in his iPod buds. I guess this conversation is over.

But as I walk up the stairs with the tray, I'm replaying

it. *You're in charge. You're on top of it.* Just the thought gives me an inner glow. I haven't felt on top of anything for . . . for*ever.*

I tap on the door and go into my parents' room. Mum's lying in bed, her eyes closed. I think she's fallen asleep. She must have been exhausted.

I put the tray down as quietly as I can, on her dressing table. There's a bunch of framed photos on the polished wood, and I linger, looking at them all. Mum and Dad on their wedding day . . . me and Frank as babies . . . and one of Mum with all her workmates, winning some award. She's wearing a pink jacket and clutching a Perspex trophy and beaming, and she looks totally vibrant.

Mum is a freelance brand consultant, which means that she does projects all over the country. Sometimes she's really busy and sometimes she has weeks off, and that's how it's always been. She came to my school and talked about her job once, and showed us this supermarket logo redesign she'd worked on, and everyone was really impressed. I mean, she's cool. Her job is cool. Only now I'm looking at this photo I'm wondering: *When did she actually last work?*

She was on a project when I got ill. I can vaguely remember hearing her talking to Dad about it, hearing her say, "I'm pulling out. I'm not going to Manchester." All I felt then was relief. I didn't want her to go to Manchester. I didn't want her to go anywhere.

But now . . .

I look at the photo again, at Mum's happy, shiny photo face—and then down at her tired, asleep, real-life face on the bed. It hadn't occurred to me that Mum had stopped working completely. But ever since I've been at home, I realize, she hasn't gone to her office once.

I feel like I'm slowly coming out of a fog and noticing things I didn't before. What Dr. Sarah said is true: you get self-obsessed when you're ill. You can't see anything around you. But now I'm starting to see stuff.

"Audrey?"

I turn to see that Mum is pushing herself up on her elbows.

"Hi!" I say. "I thought you were asleep. I brought you some Lemsip."

Mum's face cracks into a smile, as though I've made her year.

"Sweetheart," she says. "That is *so* kind."

I bring the tray and watch as she sips the hot drink. Her face is so distant that I think she might be falling asleep again, but suddenly she focuses on me.

"Audrey," she says. "This Linus."

I feel my defenses rise at once. Not Linus. *This* Linus.

"Yes?" I say, trying to sound casual.

"Is he ...?" She trails off. "Are you ...? Is he a special friend?"

I can feel myself squirming inside. I don't want to talk about Linus to Mum.

"Kind of." I look away. "You always say I need to make friends. So. I did."

"And that's great." Mum hesitates. "But, Audrey, you need to be careful. You're vulnerable."

"Dr. Sarah says I need to push myself," I counter. "I need to begin building relationships outside the family again."

"I know." Mum looks troubled. "But I suppose I'd rather you began with . . . Well. A girl friend."

"Because girls are so nice and sweet and lovely," I retort, before I can stop myself, and Mum sighs.

"*Touché.*" She takes a sip of Lemsip, wincing. "Oh, I don't know. I suppose if this Linus is a nice boy . . ."

"He's very nice," I say firmly. "And his name isn't This Linus. It's Linus."

"What about Natalie?"

Natalie. A tiny part of me shrivels automatically at the name. But for the first time in ages, I can also feel a kind of longing. A longing for the friendship we had. For friendship, full stop.

There's quiet in the room as I try to pick through my muddled thoughts. Mum doesn't push me. She knows it sometimes takes me a long time to work out what I think. She's pretty patient.

I feel like I've been on this massive long, lonely journey, and none of my friends could ever understand it, even Natalie. I think I kind of hated them for that. But now everything's feeling easier. Maybe I could see Natalie sometime? Maybe we could hang out? Maybe it wouldn't matter that she can't understand what I've been through?

There's a photo on Mum's dressing table of Natalie and me dressed up for last year's Year 9 prom, and I find my eyes swiveling towards it. Nat's in a pink lacy dress and I'm in blue. We're laughing and pulling party poppers. We did that picture about six times to get the party poppers just right. They were Nat's idea. She has funny ideas like that. I mean, she does make you laugh, Nat.

"Maybe I will call Natalie," I say at last. "Sometime." I look at Mum for a reaction, but she's fallen asleep. The half-full Lemsip is tilting dangerously on the tray, and I grab it before it can spill. I leave it on her bedside table in case she wakes up, then tiptoe out of the room and head downstairs, full of a kind of new energy.

"Frank," I demand as I enter the kitchen. "Has Mum given up work?"

"Yeah, I think so."

"For good?"

"Dunno."

"But she's really good at her job."

"Yes, but she can't go out, can she?"

He doesn't say it, but I know what he means. *Because of you.*

Because of me, Mum is hanging around at home, worrying and reading the *Daily Mail*. Because of me, Mum looks all tense and tired instead of shiny and happy.

"She should work. She likes work."

Frank shrugs. "Well. I expect she will. You know . . ."

And again, the unspoken hangs in the air: *When you get better.*

"I'll go and get the grapes," he says, and ambles out of the kitchen. And I sit, staring at my blurry reflection in the stainless steel fridge. When I get better. Well then. It's up to me to get better.

INTERIOR. 5 ROSEWOOD CLOSE. DAY

Dad is making a call at his desk in the study.

> ### DAD
> (into phone)
> Yes. Yup. I'll check that. (He taps at
> the computer.) OK, I've got it up now.

Frank barges into the room without knocking.

> ### FRANK
> Dad, I need to look something up for my
> geography homework.

> ### DAD
> You'll have to do it later.
> Sorry, Mark—

> ### FRANK
> But I can't do my homework till I look
> this up.

> ### DAD
> Frank, do it later.

Frank looks at him, wide-eyed.

> ### FRANK
> You always tell me to prioritize my
> homework. You always say, "Don't put off
> your homework, Frank." But now you're
> telling me to put off my homework. I
> mean, isn't that mixed messages? Aren't
> parents supposed to be consistent?

                    DAD
                  (sighs)
          Fine. Look it up. Mark, I'll call you
          back.

He gives way to Frank at the computer. Frank taps a
few times, looks at a website, and scribbles something
down.

                    FRANK
          Thanks.

As Frank leaves, Dad redials and summons up his
document on the computer.

                    DAD
          Sorry, Mark. So, as I was saying, these
          figures really don't make sense—

He stops as Frank comes in again.

                    FRANK
          I need to look up the population of
          Uruguay.

Dad puts his hand over the phone.

                    DAD
          What?

                    FRANK
          Uruguay. Population.

Dad stares at him, exasperated.

                    DAD
          Is this really essential right now?

Frank looks hurt.

                              FRANK

          It's for my homework, Dad. You always
          say, what I do at school will affect my
          whole life. I mean I would do it on my
          own computer, but . . . well.
                    (He looks sombrely at the floor.)
          That was Mum's decision. We'll never know
          why she did what she did.

                               DAD

          Frank—

                              FRANK

          No, it's OK. If you want to put your
          phone call above my education then
          that's your decision.

                               DAD
                             (snaps)
          Fine. Look it up. (He gets up.) Mark,
          we'll have to do this much later. Sorry.

                              FRANK
                        (at the computer)
          It should be on histories . . .

     He summons up a page entitled Financing Your Alfa
     Romeo.

                              FRANK

          Wow, Dad. Are you buying an Alfa Romeo?
          Does Mum know?

                               DAD
                             (snaps)
          That is private. That is nothing—

He breaks off as he sees Frank tapping at the
keyboard.

>   DAD
>   Frank, what are you doing? What's
>   happened to my screen?

Dad's bland, seaside wallpaper has been replaced by a
leering graphic character from *LOC*.

>   FRANK
>   You needed a new wallpaper. Your one
>   was rank. Now we need some new sound
>   settings . . .

He clicks the mouse and *Boomshakalaka* blasts from the
computer.

Dad completely loses it.

>   DAD
>   Stop that! That is *my* computer . . .
>   (He gets up and stalks to the door.)
>   Anne? Anne?

<u>MY SERENE AND LOVING FAMILY—FILM TRANSCRIPT</u>

INTERIOR. 5 ROSEWOOD CLOSE. DAY.

From the door of the kitchen, we can see Dad and Mum, having a low-pitched fight.

                    DAD

          He needs his own computer. We can't
          share anymore. I'll end up murdering him.

                    MUM

          He does not *need* a computer!

                    DAD

          He needs it for his homework. All the
          kids do.

                    MUM

          Rubbish.

                    DAD

          It's not! You know they take notes on
          laptops these days? They don't even know
          what pens are for. They think they're
          styluses which are somehow leaking a
          weird substance. I mean, they can't
          write anymore. Forget writing.

                    MUM

          What are you saying? That children *need*
          computers? That it's physically impossible
          to learn anything without a computer? What
          about books? What about libraries?

                    DAD

          When did you last go to a library?
          They're full of computers. That's how
          people learn these days.

                              MUM
                          (outraged)
          Are you telling me that in the African
          scrubland, children can't learn to read
          unless they have a computer? Are you
          telling me that?

                              DAD
                          (baffled)
          African scrubland? When did the African
          scrubland come into it?

                              MUM
          Do you need a computer to read great
          literature?

                              DAD
          Actually, I'm really getting into my
          Kindle—

He sees Mum's face.

                              DAD
          I mean, no. Definitely not.

MY SERENE AND LOVING FAMILY—FILM TRANSCRIPT

INTERIOR. 5 ROSEWOOD CLOSE. DAY.

A hand knocks at Frank's door.

> **FRANK**
> Who is it?

> **AUDREY (VOICE-OVER)**
> Me!

> **FRANK**
> OK.

The door opens and the camera proceeds jerkily into the room. It is a tip of teenage stuff. Frank is sitting by the window, playing a game on a 1980s Atari console. Bleepy, tinny noises fill the room.

> **AUDREY (V.O.)**
> You could have looked up Uruguay on your phone.

> **FRANK**
> Yeah.

> **AUDREY (V.O.)**
> So you're just messing with Dad.

> **FRANK**
> I need a computer.

The camera focuses on the Atari console.

> **AUDREY (V.O.)**
> Where did you find that?

                              FRANK

            In the loft.

There's a knock at the door and, in one seamless
motion, Frank throws a tracksuit over the Atari
console, swivels his chair round, and picks up a book.

Mum comes in and looks around the room.

                               MUM

            Frank, this room is a mess. You need to
            tidy it up.

Frank shrugs.

                               MUM

            So what are you up to?

                              FRANK

            Just . . . you know.

He glances at the camera.

                              FRANK

            The usual.

I'm doing it. I'm getting better. Not just baby-steps better, massive-great-strides better. It's three weeks later and I'm feeling more on top of it than ever. I've been to Starbucks three times, Costa once, and The Ginger Biscuit once for milk shakes. I know! Dr. Sarah was like, "Audrey, you are making strides!" Then she told me not to go too fast too soon, yadda yadda, but you could tell she was impressed.

I've even had lunch at a pizza restaurant! I had to leave before pudding because the restaurant suddenly got too clattery and threatening—but still, I lasted a whole Quattro Staggioni. Mum and Dad came too, and Linus and Frank and Felix, and it felt like we were . . . you know. A normal group. Apart from the fact that one of us was sitting there in dark glasses like some sad, wannabe celeb. I said that to Mum and she said, "You think you're the abnormal-looking one? Look at Felix!"

Which was a fair point, as Felix was dressed in his beloved new morph suit with a tiger mask on top of it, and had a tantrum when we pointed out that he wouldn't be able to eat any pizza like that.

So that made me feel better. In fact, a lot is making me feel better at the moment. Seeing Linus is definitely making me feel better. We text all the time and he comes over every day after school, and we've started playing table tennis in the garden, like, obsessively. Even Frank joins in sometimes.

And today was amazing, because Linus gave me a present. A T-shirt. It has a picture of rhubarb on it and he got it off the Internet. Mum and Dad said "Why rhubarb?" and he winked at me and said, "It's our thing."

Our thing.

I'm not sure what makes me happier—the T-shirt or the *our thing*. I've never had an *our thing* with a boy before. Whichever it is, I'm still glowing. Mum and Dad are out and Frank is doing homework and Felix is in bed and I feel fired up. I feel restless. I'm wandering around the house in my T-shirt, feeling like I want to share all this. I want to talk to someone. I want to see someone

Natalie. I want to see Natalie.

The thought is like a light ray in my brain, so positive, it makes me blink. I want to see her. I want my friend back. Yes. I'm going to do it. Right now.

I've nearly phoned Nat a couple of times since I had that talk with Mum. Once I was actually halfway through dialling when I chickened out at the last moment. But today I can face it. I can more than face it.

I get out my phone and key in Natalie's number before I can change my mind. I know it off by heart, even though I haven't spoken to her for, like, a zillion years. The last time we saw each other was on that awful last day at school, and she was crying, and I was, like, beyond crying, and it wasn't the greatest goodbye.

I text:

> Hi Nat. How are u? I'm a lot better. Love to c u sometime. Auds. x

About thirty seconds later her reply arrives. It's like she's been sitting by her phone all this time, all these weeks, waiting.

Which maybe she has. I blink at the text, which goes like this:

> OMG Auds. I have been SO WORRIED ABOUT U. Can I come round? Shall I come round now? Mum says it's fine. Nat xxxxx

I text back:

> OK C u soon.

And what seems like five minutes later, the doorbell rings. It might have been ten minutes. It definitely wasn't any longer than that. She must have left the house that exact second.

I swing open the front door and step back, a bit unnerved. Not because I'm not pleased to see Natalie, but because of all the stuff she's holding. She's got a gift basket of bath oil and a teddy bear holding a banner saying *Get Well Soon* and some books and magazines and bars of chocolate and a massive card.

"Hi," I say faintly. "Wow."

"We wanted to visit you before," says Nat in a rush. "But your mum said . . ." She swallows. "Anyway. So we'd already bought all this stuff. It's just been sitting there in the hall." She looks at her laden arms. "I know. It looks a bit mad."

"Well . . . come in."

As she edges in, she's eyeing up my dark glasses until I say, "What is it?"

"People at school told me they'd seen you in those." She points at my dark glasses. "You know, in the street. Even when it's raining. No-one knows why you wear them all the time."

"It's just . . . you know." I shrug awkwardly. "Being ill and everything."

"Oh." She seems a bit freaked out. "Right."

She comes in and dumps the stuff on the kitchen table and looks at me. For a moment there's a prickly, awkward silence, except the ticking of the clock, and I think *Was this a mistake?*

I'm tense like a cat. I'm wary. It's not the way I expected to be, but seeing Nat is bringing back all kinds of things I'd put away in my mind.

"I'm sorry." Her voice comes out in a miserable gush. "Auds, I'm sorry, I'm so sorry—"

"No." I shake my head, not wanting to go there. "You don't have to be sorry."

"But I should've— I didn't—" Tears are trickling down her face. "I still can't believe it happened."

"It's OK. Look, have a drink."

I pour us both some elderflower. I should have realized she'd be upset. In my head I've skipped past all that. Or trudged through it, more like. *Worked through it,* is what Dr. Sarah would say. *Processed it.* Like I'm a cheese slice machine.

I don't think Nat has processed an awful lot. Every time she looks at me, fresh tears pour down her face.

"And now you're ill."

"I'm fine. I'm a lot better. I've got a boyfriend!"

OK, that sounded a bit abrupt, but let's face it—this *was* the main purpose of inviting her over. To tell her I've got a boyfriend. Immediately her tears vanish and she leans forward, avidly.

"A boyfriend? From the hospital?"

FFS. What does she think, that I'm some mental case hanging out with another mental case because that's all I'm fit for now?

"No, not from the hospital," I say impatiently. "It's Linus. You know? In Frank's year at Cardinal Nicholls?"

"Linus? You mean ... Atticus Finch?" Nat seems flabbergasted.

"Exactly. He gave me this." I point at my T-shirt. "Today. Isn't it cool?"

"Is that a picture of rhubarb?" She looks confused.

"Yes. It's our thing," I say casually.

"Wow." Nat seems unable to get over this news. "So ... how long have you been going out?"

"A few weeks. We go to Starbucks and stuff. I mean, it's just ... you know. Kind of fun."

"I thought you were, like, properly ill. Like, in bed."

"Well, I was." I shrug. "I suppose I'm recovering or whatever." I rip open a bar of chocolate and break it into pieces. "So, tell me about school."

I force myself to ask it, even though the word *school* leaves a nasty sensation in my brain; a kind of poisonous imprint.

"Oh, everything's different now," says Natalie vaguely. "You wouldn't believe it. Now that Tasha and that lot have left. Katie's *totally* changed. You wouldn't even know her. And Chloe isn't friends with Ruby anymore, and you know Miss Moore left? Well, we have a new deputy head now and she's brilliant—" Natalie breaks off from her jabbering. "So, are you going to come back?"

The question hits me like a punch in the stomach. The idea of going back to that place literally makes me feel ill.

"I'm going to the Heath Academy," I tell her. "I'm going to go down a year, because I've missed so much school time. I mean, I'm young for the year anyway, so it'll all work out . . ."

"You could go down a year at Stokeland?" suggests Nat, but I wrinkle my nose.

"That would be weird. To be in the year below you. Anyway . . ." I pause. "They hate us at Stokeland. My parents got really angry with them. They called this whole big governors' meeting and had a go at them and it all got . . . you know. Acrimonious." I know this from Frank, *not* from Mum and Dad. "They reckon the staff didn't handle things well."

"Well, they didn't!" Nat opens her eyes wide. "Everyone says that the whole time. Like, my parents go on about it."

"Well. So. Exactly. It'd be weird to come back."

I break the chocolate into more pieces and offer them to Nat. She takes a piece, then looks up, a tear trickling down her face again. "I miss you, Auds."

"I miss you too."

"It was really horrible when you'd gone. *Really* horrible."

"Yeah."

There's a moment's pause—then somehow, with no warning, we're hugging one other. Natalie smells of Herbal Essences, just like she always does, and she has this little thing of patting you in the small of your back which brings tears to my eyes, just because it's so familiar.

I've missed hugging. *God*, I've missed hugging.

As we draw away from each other, we're both laughing but a bit teary too. Natalie's phone rings and she grabs it impatiently.

"Yes, Mum," she says shortly. "Everything's *fine*. That's Mum," she explains as she throws her phone down again. "She's waiting outside in the car. I was supposed to text her every five minutes to say everything's OK."

"Why?"

"Because . . . you know."

"What?"

"You know." Natalie wriggles awkwardly, looking past me.

"I don't."

"Auds. *You* know. Because you're . . ."

"What?"

"Mentally unstable," says Natalie, practically in a whisper.

"What?" I stare at her, genuinely gobsmacked. "What do you mean?"

"You're bipolar." Natalie's cringing all over. "Bipolar people can become violent. Mum was just worried."

"I'm not *bipolar*!" I say in astonishment. "Who told you I was bipolar?"

"Aren't you?" Natalie's jaw drops open. "Well, Mum said you must be bipolar."

"So I'm going to attack you? Because I should never have been let out of my institution and should in fact be in a straitjacket? Jesus!" I try to stay calm. "I've met bipolar people, Nat, and they were perfectly safe, believe it or not."

"Look, I'm sorry!" Natalie looks unhappy. "But we didn't know, did we?"

"Didn't my mum *tell* you what was wrong? Didn't she explain?"

"Well . . ." Natalie looks still more awkward. "My mum thought she was putting a gloss on it. I mean, there have been all these rumours—"

"Like what? What rumours?" Natalie is silent, and I put on my most menacing tone. "What rumours, Nat?"

"OK!" she says hurriedly. "Like you tried to commit suicide . . . like you've gone blind . . . like you can't speak anymore . . . Oh! Someone said you'd gouged out your own eyes and that's why you wear dark glasses."

"What?" I feel winded from shock. "And you *believed* them?"

"No!" Natalie looks foolish. "Of course I didn't believe them. But—"

"I gouged out my own eyes? Like Van Gogh?"

"That was ears," Natalie points out. "Only one ear."

"I *gouged out my own eyes*?" I feel a bit hysterical. A

weird, painful laughter is bubbling through me. "You believed it, didn't you, Nat? You believed it."

"I didn't!" Natalie is getting all pink. "Of course I didn't. I'm just telling you!"

"But you thought I was a bipolar homicidal maniac."

"I don't even know what bipolar means," admits Natalie. "I mean, it's just one of those words."

"A bipolar, homicidal maniac with gouged-out eyes." I feel a fresh wave of hysteria. "No wonder your mum's outside in the car."

"Stop it!" wails Natalie. "I didn't mean any of it!"

Natalie is a total, utter dope and her mum is worse. But I can't help feeling a wave of affection as I watch her, all miserable and flustered and not knowing what to say. I've known Nat since we were six, and even then she was totally wide-eyed and thought my dad really was Father Christmas.

"I'm fine," I say at last, letting Natalie off the hook. "It's fine. Don't worry about it."

"Really?" Natalie looks at me anxiously. "Oh God, Auds, I'm sorry. You *know* I don't know anything about anything." She bites her lip, thinking for a moment. "So . . . if you're not bipolar, what are you?"

The question takes me by surprise. I have to think for a few seconds before I reply.

"I'm getting better," I say at last. "That's what I am." I reach for the last piece of the chocolate bar and split it into two. "C'mon. Let's finish this before Frank sees it."

Dr. Sarah loves the bipolar homicidal maniac story.

Well, I say "loves." She actually groans and clutches her hair with both hands and says "Seriously?" And I can see her writing *Outreach program—schools? EDUCATE???* on her notepad.

But I just laugh. I mean, it *is* funny, even if it's all wrong too. You have to see that.

I laugh a lot more when I see Dr. Sarah these days. And I talk a *lot* more. For a long time it seemed like she had more to say than I did. It seemed like she did most of the talking and I did most of the listening. (To be fair, I wasn't wild about communication of any type when we first met. To be even more fair, at our first session I wouldn't even come in the room, let alone look at her, let alone speak.) But now things have flipped the other way. I have so much to tell her! About Linus, Natalie, all my trips out, that time I went on the bus and didn't panic one bit . . .

"So anyway, I reckon I'm done," I say as I finish my last story. "I'm cooked."

"Cooked?"

"Cured."

"Right." Dr. Sarah taps her pencil thoughtfully. "Which means . . ."

"You know. I'm fine. Back to normal."

"You're certainly making very good progress. I'm delighted, Audrey. Really delighted."

"No, not just 'good progress,'" I say impatiently. "I'm back to normal. I mean, you know. Practically."

"Mmhhm." Dr. Sarah always leaves a polite pause before she contradicts me. "You haven't been back to school yet," she points out. "You're still wearing dark glasses. You're still on medication."

"OK, I said 'practically.'" I feel a spike of anger. "You don't have to be so negative."

"Audrey, I just need you to be realistic."

"I am!"

"Remember the graph of your progress that I drew? The jagged line?"

"Yes, well, that graph is old news," I say. "This is my graph."

I stand up, march to the white board and draw a straight line, zooming up to the stars. "This is me. No more down. Only up."

Dr. Sarah sighs. "Audrey, I'd love that to be true. But the overwhelming majority of patients recovering from an episode such as yours will encounter setbacks. And that's fine. It's normal."

"Well, I've had all my setbacks." I look at her stonily. "I've done setbacks, OK? I'm just not having any more. It's not happening."

"I know you're frustrated, Audrey—"

"I'm thinking positive. What's wrong with that?"

"Nothing. Just don't overdo it. Don't put pressure on yourself. The danger is that you give yourself a *real* setback."

"I'm fine," I say resolutely.

"Yes, you are." She nods. "But you're also fragile. Imagine a mended china plate which hasn't quite set."

"I'm a *plate*?" I say sardonically, but Dr. Sarah doesn't rise to it.

"I had a patient a few years ago, very similar to you, Audrey, who was at the same stage of her recovery. She decided to go to Disneyland Paris, against my advice." She rolls her eyes. "Disneyland! Of all places!"

Even the idea of Disneyland makes me wince, not that I'll admit that to Dr. Sarah.

"What happened?" I can't resist asking.

"It was far too much for her. She had to come home from the trip early. Then she felt she'd failed. Her mood sank to the lowest it had been, and it didn't do her progress any good."

"Well, I won't go to Disneyland." I fold my arms. "So."

"Good. I know you're sensible." As Dr. Sarah surveys me, her mouth twitches. "You've got your spirit back, at any rate. And life is good?"

"Life is good."

"And Linus is still . . ." She pauses delicately.

"Linus." I nod. "He's still Linus. He says hi, by the way."

"Oh!" Dr. Sarah seems taken aback. "Well, say hi back."

"And he says, 'Good job.'"

There's silence and a little smile creeps round Dr. Sarah's face. "Well," she says. "You can say that back to him too. I'd like to meet this Linus."

"Yeah, well, don't get your hopes up," I say with a deadpan shrug. "He's mine."

MY SERENE AND LOVING FAMILY——FILM TRANSCRIPT

INTERIOR. 5 ROSEWOOD CLOSE. DAY.

LONG SHOT: Linus and FELIX are sitting in the garden.
They have a chessboard between them and appear to be
playing chess.

The camera pans closer and their voices become audible.

Felix moves a piece and looks triumphantly at Linus.

> **FELIX**
> Chess.

Linus moves a piece.

> **LINUS**
> Chess.

Felix moves a piece.

> **FELIX**
> Chess.

Linus moves a piece.

> **LINUS**
> Chess.

He looks at Felix seriously.

> **LINUS**
> This is a good game you invented, Felix.

Felix beams at him.

> **FELIX**
> I know.

                         LINUS
          What do you call it again?

                         FELIX
          Squares.

Linus is struggling to keep a straight face.

                         LINUS
          That's right. Squares. So why don't we
          say "Squares" when we move the pieces?

Felix looks at him pityingly, as though he's a little dim.

                         FELIX
          Because we say "Chess."

Linus looks at the camera.

                         LINUS
          That tells me.

Mum comes into the garden.

                         MUM
          Linus! You're here! Marvellous. Now,
          you speak German, don't you?

                         LINUS
                      (warily)
          A bit.

                         MUM
          Great! Well, you can come and help me
          decipher my new dishwasher instructions.
          The whole leaflet's in German. I mean,
          German. I ask you.

                         LINUS
          Oh. OK.

As he gets up, Felix grabs onto his leg.

                    FELIX
          Lin-us! Play Squares!

At this moment, Frank comes into the garden and
brandishes a gaming magazine at Linus.

                    FRANK
          Linus, you have to see this.

              AUDREY (VOICE-OVER)
          What is this family LIKE? Stop trying
          to kidnap my boyfriend, everyone. OK?

Dr. Sarah has said I need to increase my interactions with strangers. It's not enough just to go to a restaurant and hide behind a menu and let other people order for me. (How did she guess?) I need to talk confidently to unfamiliar people. This is my homework. So Linus and I are sitting in Starbucks and he's choosing someone random for me to go and talk to.

We did all kinds of role-play in hospital, which was supposed to achieve the same aim. But role-play is role-play. You feel so *stupid.* OMG it was embarrassing, pretending to have a "confrontation" with some skinny boy who you knew would practically go into a panic attack if you even looked at him. And all the counsellors having to feed us lines when we dried up, and saying "Look at your body language, Audrey."

Anyway. So role-play totally sucks, but this is kind of fun. Because I'm going to do one and then Linus is going to do one. It's like dares.

"OK, that guy." Linus points to a man on his own at a corner table, who's tapping away at a laptop. He's in his twenties with a goatee and has a grey T-shirt and one of those cool leather man-bags that Frank despises. "Go up to that guy and ask him if he has Wi-Fi."

I feel a bubble of panic, which I try to swallow down. The man looks absorbed in his work. He doesn't look like he wants to be interrupted.

"He looks really busy . . ." I prevaricate. "What about someone else? What about that old lady?" There's a sweet-looking, grey-haired woman sitting at the next table, who has already smiled in our direction.

"Too easy." Linus is adamant. "You won't need to say a word, she'll just jabber at you. Go up to that guy and ask about the Wi-Fi. I'll wait here."

Everything in my body is telling me not to go, but Linus is sitting there looking at me, so I force my leg muscles to operate. Somehow I'm walking across the coffee shop and now I'm standing right in front of the man, but he hasn't looked at me. He's just tapping and frowning.

"Um, hi?" I manage.

Tap-tap-tap-frown.

"Hi?" I try again.

Tap-tap-tap-frown. He hasn't even looked up.

I so want to back away. But Linus is watching. I have to see this through.

"Excuse me?" My voice bursts out so loudly I almost jump in fright, and finally the man lifts his head. "I was wondering if you have Wi-Fi?"

"What?" He scowls.

"Wi-Fi? Do you have Wi-Fi here?"

"Jesus. I'm trying to *work*."

"Right. Sorry. I was just wondering—"

"About the Wi-Fi. Are you blind? Can you read, at all?" He points to a notice in the corner of the coffee shop, which is all about the Starbucks Wi-Fi code. Then he focuses on my dark glasses. "*Are* you blind? Or just subnormal?"

"I'm not blind," I say, my voice trembling. "I was just asking. Sorry to bother you."

"Fucking moron," he mutters as he starts tapping again.

Tears are welling in my eyes, and as I back away, my legs are wobbly. But my chin is high. I'm determined I'm not going to dissolve. As I get back to the table, I force a kind of rictus grin onto my face.

"I did it!"

"What did he say?" demands Linus.

"He called me a fucking moron. And blind and subnormal. Apart from that, you know, he was really charming."

The tears in my eyes are edging down my cheeks by now, and Linus stares at them in alarm.

"Audrey!"

"No, I'm fine," I say fiercely. "I'm fine."

"Wanker." Linus is glaring balefully at the man in the grey T-shirt. "If he doesn't want to be disturbed, he shouldn't come and sit in a public place. You realize how much he's saving on rent? He buys one coffee and sits there for an hour and then he expects the whole world to tiptoe around him. If he wants an office he should pay for an office. Fucker."

"Anyway, I did it." I speak brightly. "Your turn now."

"I'm speaking to the same guy." Linus gets to his feet. "He doesn't get away with being such a prick."

"What are you going to say?" I ask in panic. A choking dread is filling my chest, and I don't even know what I'm scared of. I just don't want Linus to go over there. I want to leave. "Sit down," I beg him. "Let's stop the game."

"The game hasn't finished." Linus winks at me and heads over to the corner table, coffee in hand. "Hi!" he says to the man in a childish voice which is so loud that half the coffee shop looks round. "That's an Apple Mac, isn't it?"

The man looks up as though in disbelief at being interrupted again.

"Yes," he says curtly.

"Could you tell me the advantages of an Apple Mac over other brands of computer?" says Linus. "Because I want to buy a computer. Is your one really good? I bet it is." He sits down opposite the man. "Can I have a go?"

"Look, I'm busy," the man snaps. "Could you sit somewhere else?"

"Are you working here?"

There's silence as the man continues tapping and Linus leans forward. "Are you working?" he repeats in a foghorn voice.

"Yes!" The man glowers at him. "I'm working."

"My dad works in an office," says Linus artlessly. "Don't you have an office? What do you do? Could I be like your shadow? Will you come and give a talk to our school? Oh look, your cup's empty. Are you going to buy another coffee? Was that a cappuccino? I like flat whites. But why are they called flat whites? Do you know? Can you look it up for me?"

"Listen." The man slams his laptop shut. "Kid. I'm working. Could you please find another table?"

"But this is Starbucks," says Linus in tones of surprise.

"You can sit anywhere. You're allowed." He flags down a female barista who's collecting empty cups nearby. "Excuse me, can I sit anywhere? Is that how Starbucks works?"

"Of course," says the barista, and smiles at him. "Anywhere you like."

"Did you hear that? Anywhere I like. And I've got a cup of coffee, but you haven't," Linus points out to the man. "You've finished yours. Hey, wait." He gives the empty cup to the barista. "See?" he says to the man. "You're all done. You should either buy a cup of coffee or go."

"Jesus!" Looking like he wants to explode, the man shoves his laptop into his man-bag and gets to his feet.

"Fucking *kids*," he mutters to himself. "*Unbelievable.*"

"Bye then," says Linus innocently. "Have fun being a wanker."

For an instant I think the man might hit him round the head—but of course he doesn't. He just heads out of the coffee shop looking savage. Linus gets up and slides back into the seat opposite me, his face all creased up into his orange segment smile.

"Oh my God." I exhale. "I can't believe you did that."

"Next time, you do it."

"I couldn't!"

"You could. It's fun." Linus rubs his hands together. "Bring it on."

"OK, give me another one," I say, inspired. "Give me another dare."

"Ask this barista if they serve mint muffins. Go." He flags her down, and she comes over with a smile. I haven't even got time to think about whether I'm nervous or not.

"Excuse me, do you serve mint muffins?" I say, adopting Linus's innocent, childlike tones. Somehow, channelling Linus is giving me strength. I'm not me, I'm not Audrey, I'm a character.

"Ah, no." She shakes her head. "I'm sorry."

"But I saw them on the website," I say. "I'm sure I saw them. Mint muffins with a chocolate centre? With, like, sprinkles?"

"And Polo mints on top," chimes in Linus seriously, and I nearly crease up with laughter.

"No." The barista looks puzzled. "I never heard of them."

"Oh well," I say politely, "thank you anyway." As she walks off, I grin at Linus, feeling a bit heady. "I did it!"

"You can talk to anyone." He nods. "Next, why don't you hire a soapbox and make a speech?"

"Great idea!" I say. "Let's invite, like, a thousand people."

"So the graph is going upwards. Miss Audrey is heading for the stars." Linus knows about the jagged/not-jagged graph, because I told him about it. I drew it out and everything.

"Definitely." I clink my coffee cup against his. "Miss Audrey is heading for the stars."

Which just proves it: I'm in charge of my graph. *Me*. And if I want a straight graph, I'll have a straight graph.

So at my next session with Dr. Sarah, I lie a little when I'm filling in my tick boxes.

Have you experienced worries most days? Not at all.

Do you find your worries difficult to control? Not at all.

She looks at the sheet with raised eyebrows when I hand it to her.

"Well. This is an improvement!"

"You see?" I can't help saying at once. "You see?"

"Do you have any idea why you've improved so much this week, Audrey?" She smiles at me. "Life's good, is it just that? Or anything else? Any changes?"

"Dunno." I shrug innocently. "I can't think of anything that's changed in particular."

Which is another lie. Something that's changed is: I've

stopped taking my meds. I just take the pills out of the blister packs and chuck them away in a screwed-up envelope. (Not down the loo, because all the chemicals get into the water or whatever.)

And guess what? I haven't noticed a single difference. Which just proves I didn't need them.

I haven't told anybody. Well, obviously I haven't, because they'd stress out. I'm going to wait, like, a month and then I'll casually tell everyone and I'll be like, you *see*?

"I told you," I say to Dr. Sarah. "I'm cooked. I'm done. All better."

Mum's in an organizing mood. She's sweeping around the house, tidying and shouting and saying "Whose shoes are these? What are they *doing* here?" and we've all hidden in the garden. I mean me, Frank, Linus, and Felix. It's a warm day anyway, so it's nice, just sitting on the grass, picking daisies.

There's a rustling sound, and Dad appears round the side of the bush we're lurking behind.

"Hi, Dad," says Frank. "Have you come to join the Rebel Alliance?"

"Frank, I think your mother wants you," says Dad.

Your mother. Code for: *Don't associate me with Mum's latest nutty plan, I have nothing to do with it.*

"Why?" Frank gives an unpromising scowl. "I'm busy."

"Busy hiding behind a bush?" I say, and snort with laughter.

"You offered to help?" Dad says. "For the Avonlea fete catering? I think they're starting."

"I did not offer to help," says Frank, looking outraged. "I did not *offer.* I was forced. This is forced labour."

"You have such a great attitude," I observe. "Helping your fellow man and everything."

"I don't notice *you* helping your fellow man," Frank shoots back.

"I'll help my fellow man." I shrug. "I don't mind making a few sandwiches."

"Anyway, fellow *man?*" counters Frank. "That's sexist. Glad you're such a sexist, Audrey."

"It's an expression."

"It's a sexist expression."

"I think we should go," Dad cuts in. "Mum's on the warpath."

"I'm entertaining Linus," says Frank, without moving an inch. "I'm entertaining a guest. You want me to abandon my guest?"

"He's *my* guest," I object.

"He was my friend first." Frank glowers at me.

"I have to go anyway," says Linus diplomatically. "Water polo practice."

After Linus leaves, we hear Mum yelling, "Chris! Frank! Where *are* you!" in her most ominous You'll-pay-for-this-later voice and it's like we all realize there's no point hiding out here anymore. Frank trudges back to the house looking like a condemned man and I take a few deep breaths because I'm feeling a little edgy.

I mean, I'm fine. I'm not panicking or anything. I'm just a tiny bit—

Well. A bit jittery. Dunno why. I'm probably just getting back to normal after all those months polluting my body with chemicals. I mean, when is the last time I knew what normal even *was*?

The kitchen is full of the most motley crew of people. There's one old lady in an ancient purple suit and hair which is clearly a wig. There's one middle-aged lady with plaits and sandals. There's a plump couple who are wearing matching St. Luke's Church sweatshirts. And a white-haired man on a mobility scooter.

The mobility scooter's pretty cool, actually. But it *is* kind of getting in everyone's way.

"Right!" Mum comes in and claps her hands. "Welcome, everybody, and thank you for coming along today. So, the fete starts at three. I've bought lots of ingredients . . ." She starts emptying food out of supermarket carriers onto the kitchen table—stuff like tomatoes and cucumbers, lettuce and bread, chicken and ham. "I thought we could make some sandwiches, stuffed wraps, um . . . does anyone have any other ideas?"

"Sausage rolls?" says the plump woman.

"Right." Mum nods. "D'you mean buy sausage rolls or make sausage rolls?"

"Ooh." The plump woman looks baffled. "I don't know. But people like sausage rolls."

"Well, we haven't got any sausage rolls. Or any sausage meat. So—"

"That's a shame," says the plump woman. "Because people like sausage rolls."

Her husband nods. "They do."

"Everyone loves a sausage roll."

I can see Mum getting a little tense. "Maybe next time,"

she says brightly. "Moving on. So, I thought . . . egg sand-wiches?"

"Mum!" Frank says in horror. "Egg sandwiches are rank."

"I like egg sandwiches!" says Mum defensively. "Does anyone else like egg sandwiches?"

"Sweetheart, I think we can do better than egg sand-wiches." A man's voice cuts across Mum's, and we all look up. A bloke I've never seen before is striding into the kitchen. He must be in his twenties. He's got a shaved head and about six earrings in one ear and is wearing one of those chef outfits.

"I'm Ade," he announces. "My grandad's Derek Gould—he just moved into Avonlea. Told me about this. What are we doing?"

"Are you a chef?" Mum goggles at him. "A *professional* chef?"

"I work at the Fox and Hounds. I've got an hour. This what you've got?" He's turning Mum's food over in his hands. "I think we can knock up some nice fresh fillings to go in the wraps, maybe a Waldorf salad, maybe roast this fennel off and do it with a lemon-tarragon dressing . . ."

"Young man." Purple lady waves a hand in his face. "How will we keep salads fresh on a day like today?"

Ade looks surprised. "Oh, I brought the chill boxes from the pub. Thirty. And all the other catering supplies. You can give them back tomorrow."

The purple lady blinks at him in surprise.

"Chill boxes?" Mum is starting to look overexcited. "Ca-tering supplies? You're a saint!"

"No problemo. OK, so our menu is Waldorf salad wrap, Mexican bean wrap, a couple of salads—"

"Um, could we use some eggs?" says Mum, looking embarrassed. "I bought a whole load of eggs for egg sandwiches, which no-one seems keen on."

"Spanish omelette," says Ade without missing a beat. "We'll put in some chorizo, garlic, fry off some sweet onion, serve it in slices . . ."

I *love* Spanish omelette. This guy is so cool!

"I bought lots of peppers too," says Mum eagerly, handing him one. "Could they go in?"

"Perfect."

Ade takes the pepper from Mum and turns it over in his fingers. Then he opens up his back pack to reveal a set of knives, all carefully packed in covers. We watch agog as he takes a chopping board from the kitchen table, places the pepper on it, and starts chopping it up.

Oh my God, I have *never* seen anyone chop so fast.

Chop-chop-chop-chop-chop.

Everyone in the kitchen is just staring in astonishment. Even Frank. In fact, especially Frank. When Ade finishes and everyone bursts into applause, Frank is the only one who is still transfixed, his eyes like saucers.

"You." Ade seems to notice him. "I want you on dicing duty."

"But . . ." Frank swallows. "I can't do that."

"I'll teach you. No sweat." Ade looks Frank up and down. "You cooking in that? Got an apron?"

"I can find one," says Frank hastily, and I stifle a giggle. Frank's going to wear an *apron*?

Ade is now rootling around in Mum's cupboards, dumping ingredients all over the counter.

"I'm going to make a shopping list," he announces. "We need Parmesan, more garlic, harissa . . . Who's our runner?" He looks at me. "Pretty girl in the dark glasses. You want to be our runner?"

◆ ◆ ◆

Shopping's OK-ish for me now.

I mean, it's not always *easy*. I still have to deal with my lizard brain, which springs into action whenever I don't want it to. Over the last few days, I've been feeling these, like, waves of panic at random times, which is really annoying, because I thought I'd got rid of them.

But what I've learned is not to *fight* my lizard brain, but kind of *tolerate* it. Listen to it and then say, "Yeah, whatever." Just like you tolerate a four-year-old. I've come to think of my lizard brain as basically a version of Felix. It's totally random and makes no sense and you can't let it run your life. If we let Felix run our lives, we'd all wear superhero costumes all day long and eat nothing but ice-cream.

But if you try to fight Felix, all you get is wails and screams and tantrums, and it all gets more and more stressy. So the thing is to listen to him with half an ear and nod your head and then ignore him and do what you want to do.

Same with the lizard brain.

So when I freeze in sudden terror at the entrance to the supermarket, I force myself to smile and say, "Nice try, lizard brain." I actually say it aloud, and exhale for twelve beats. (If you breathe out really slowly, it regulates the carbon dioxide in the brain and calms you down, instantly. Try it if you don't believe me.) Then I saunter in, doing my best impression of someone who really couldn't give a toss what some old reptile thinks.

And you know what? It kind of works.

◆ ◆ ◆

When I get back home, holding two carrier bags, I stop dead in astonishment. Frank's standing at the kitchen counter, chopping.

He's wearing one of Mum's aprons and he's holding a knife I don't recognize and he's learned that cool-chef way of doing it. That chop-chop-chop thing. Fast. He's pink in the face and totally absorbed. Like, he doesn't even notice me watching, let alone come up with some wisecrack.

"Great!" Ade has noticed me and grabs the bags. "Let's get that garlic out." He sniffs it and rubs the papery skin. "Beautiful. OK, Frank, I want it finely diced. All of it."

"Yes, chef," says Frank, breathlessly, and takes the garlic.

Yes, chef?

Yes, chef?

OK, what has happened to Frank?

MY SERENE AND LOVING FAMILY—FILM TRANSCRIPT

INTERIOR. 5 ROSEWOOD CLOSE. DAY.

The camera enters the kitchen, where Frank is hunched
over Dad's laptop.

> **AUDREY (VOICE-OVER)**
> So, we had the fete today. It was OK.
> I won this in the raffle.

A hand picks up a fluffy pink loo roll cover from the
kitchen table.

> **AUDREY (V.O.)**
> You put it on your loo roll. Isn't it
> like the grossest thing you have ever
> seen?

She replaces the loo roll cover.

> **AUDREY (V.O.)**
> But everyone LOVED the food. I mean, it
> all sold out in, like, five minutes, and
> it got a special mention from the mayor.

The camera focuses in on Frank. He's watching a
YouTube video of a chef chopping.

> **FRANK**
> D'you think Mum would buy me a set of
> knives? Like, proper knives?

> **AUDREY (V.O.)**
> Dunno. How much do they cost?

Frank opens a new window on the laptop.

                    FRANK
          These ones are £650.

                 AUDREY (V.O.)
          Yup, that's really gonna happen.

                    FRANK
          You need good knives. Ade says I can
          come and learn some more skills at the
          pub. Only I have to do a bit of washing
          up or whatever, but you know, if I do
          that, he'll teach me.

He looks up, his whole face alive.

                 AUDREY (V.O.)
          That's amazing!

                    FRANK
          He has this whole thing that he does
          with a blow torch. He singes a chicken.

                 AUDREY (V.O.)
          Wow. Well, it was delicious food.
          No-one could stop talking about it.

                    FRANK
          The Waldorf needed more seasoning.
          That's what Ade said.

                 AUDREY (V.O.)
          Tasted OK to me.

The camera moves out of the kitchen and towards the
garden door. There it pauses. We see Mum and Dad,
standing by the play house, talking in low voices. Mum
is holding a letter and gesticulating furiously with
it at Dad.

                         MUM

I can't believe they would even ask this.

                         DAD

Anne, don't take it personally.

                         MUM

How can I not take it personally? How
can they have the gall? The *nerve*?

                         DAD

I know. It's preposterous.

                         MUM

It's monstrous! Do you realize how much
damage they could do to Audrey? I'm
going to email this woman tonight, and
I'm going to tell her what I think of
her and—

                         DAD

I'll send it.

                         MUM
                      (fiercely)
Well, I'm contributing. And you're NOT
censoring me, Chris.

                         DAD

We'll work out an email together. We
don't want to be too antagonistic.

                         MUM

Too antagonistic? Are you joking?

                    AUDREY (V.O.)

About what?

                          219

Both parents whip round in shock.

                    AUDREY (V.O.)
          What's going on?

                    MUM
          Audrey!

                    DAD
          It's nothing, sweetie.

                    MUM
          Nothing for you to worry about.
          Um, wasn't the fete fun?

There's a pause as the camera surveys their anxious
faces and zooms in on Mum's hand, clutching the
letter.

                    AUDREY (V.O.)
                  (slowly)
          Yes. It was super-fun.

What were they looking at? What?

I'm totally flummoxed. Mum and Dad have never been like that before. They were so anxious that I shouldn't know what they were talking about, they were kind of aggressive. I mean, Mum was almost snarly.

So whatever it is, they don't want me to have even the slightest inkling of it.

I'm nonplussed. I can't even go through all the possible theories in my head and eliminate them, because I don't have any theories. Maybe something to do with Dr. Sarah? That's all I can think of. Maybe she wants to do some weirdo experimental treatment on me and Mum and Dad are mad at her for asking?

But Dr. Sarah wouldn't do that. She wouldn't just land something like that on me. Would she? And Mum and Dad wouldn't call her *they*.

That evening at supper I bring it up again, and both Mum and Dad practically bite my head off.

"It was nothing," says Mum, eating her pasta very fast and crossly. "Nothing."

"Mum, it was something."

"You don't need to know every something in the world, Audrey."

As she says that, I feel a sudden shaft of fear—is Mum ill or something? Is there some massive family tragedy coming along to hit us like a juggernaut and that's why she won't say anything?

But no, she said *damage Audrey*. And *they*. It's all about *they*, whoever *they* are.

That evening Mum and Dad are closeted in Dad's study for, like, two hours, and then eventually they emerge, and Mum says, "Well, there we are, then." There's a kind of dark, satisfied cloud surrounding her. I have a feeling her email didn't hold back.

Dad announces he's off for a quick half with Mike who he plays squash with, and Mum says she's going to have a bath. I wait until I can hear the water running, then sidle along to Frank, who's in his room, listening to his iPod.

"Frank, can you hack into Dad's emails?" I say in a low voice.

"Yeah. Why?"

"Can we do it? Now?"

From the way Frank gets straight into Dad's inbox, it's clear he's done this before. He even knows Dad's weirdo password, which is all signs and numbers and gibberish.

"Do you often look at Dad's emails?" I say curiously, perching on the side of the office chair.

"Sometimes."

"Does he know?"

"Course not." Franks clicks on a couple of emails from someone called George Stourhead. "There's some quite interesting stuff. Did you know he applied for another job last year?"

"No."

"Didn't get it. But his mate Allan reckons the company's in trouble anyway, so Dad's well out of it."

"Oh." I digest this for a moment. "That's not interesting."

"It's better than geography coursework. Oh, and they're planning a surprise birthday party for me, so don't let on you know, OK?"

"Frank!" I wail. "Why did you tell me?"

"I didn't." He draws a line over his mouth. "I said nada. OK, what are we looking for?"

"Dunno. Some email where Mum's angry."

Frank raises his eyes so comically, I can't help giggling. "Can you narrow it down?"

"OK. Well . . . Dunno. It's about me. Search *Audrey*."

Frank gives me a funny look. "Every other email is about you, Audrey. Don't you realize that? You're Topic A in this family."

"Oh." I stare at him, taken aback. I don't know what to say to that. I don't want to be Topic A. Anyway, I'm not.

"That's rubbish," I counter. "I'm not Topic A, *you're* Topic A. All Mum talks about is you, all day long. Frank this, Frank that."

"But all she *emails* about is you. Audrey this, Audrey that." He gives me a serious look. "Believe me."

I'm silenced for a minute. I never thought of Mum having a secret email world. But of course she does. I wonder what she says. I could look. Frank could show me, I could ask him . . .

Even at the thought, it's as if a big iron gate clanks down in my mind. No. I'm not going to look. Not at anything more than is necessary. I don't want to know what Mum secretly thinks. We're all allowed our private places.

"You shouldn't spy on Mum and Dad," I say.

"You're spying too," retorts Frank.

"OK, but . . ." I wince, knowing he's right. "This is necessary. This is a one-off and it's about me and it's important and . . . I won't ever do it again."

"This'll be it, I bet." Frank is clicking on a recently sent email called *Your request*.

As the text comes up I scan straight to the bottom and it's signed from Anne and Chris Turner.

"Oh my God." Frank is chuckling. "Mum's really let this person have it."

"Shhh! Let me read it!"

I peer over his shoulder and squint at the words.

Dear Mrs. Lawton

We are writing to you in shock, horror, and dismay.
First, that you would have the nerve to write
an email directly to our daughter, Audrey, in a
completely inappropriate manner. Second, that you

should make such an outrageous request. I am sorry that your daughter Izzy is having problems, but if you think that Audrey would be willing to meet her, you must be quite mad. Do you recall the situation here? Do you recall the fact that our daughter was persecuted by your daughter (among others)? Are you aware that Audrey has not returned to school since the events and spent several weeks in hospital?

We don't care if Izzy wants to apologise or not. We are not risking any further psychological damage to our daughter.

Yours,
Anne and Chris Turner

"Who's Izzy?" says Frank. "One of them?"

"Yes." I'm getting the sick, poisoned feeling again. Just that name *Izzy* does it.

"I can't believe she wants to see me," I say, my eyes fixed on the words. "After all this time."

"Well, they said no. So you're off the hook."

"I'm not."

"You are! Look, Mum and Dad will back you up. You don't have to see anyone. Audrey, you practically don't even have to go to *school* ever again. You can do whatever the hell you like. Do you appreciate your position?" Frank clicks on another email. "You don't, do you? It's wasted on you."

I'm only barely aware of him. Thoughts are spinning

around my brain. Thoughts I don't even understand myself. Thoughts I don't want.

Without realizing I've done it, I've crumpled down on the floor and buried my head in my hands. I need all my energy for thinking.

"Aud?" Frank suddenly seems to notice. "Aud, what's up?"

"You don't understand," I say. "Reading this—knowing that they've asked—that's put me *on* the hook."

"Why?"

"Because . . ."

I can't say it. The words are in my brain, but I don't want them there. I don't know why they're there. But they won't disappear.

"Maybe I should see her." I force it out. "Maybe I should go and see her."

"What?" Frank looks aghast. "Why would you do that?"

"I don't know. Because—I don't know." I clutch my head. "I don't *know*."

"It's a crap idea," proclaims Frank. "It's like inviting bad stuff into your life. You know, it's been shit enough for you already, Aud. Don't make things worse. Hey, Dad's got a link to this quiz on *Which Simpsons character are you?*" he adds. "You should do it. Where is it . . ." Frank's clicking randomly all over the desktop. "Dad's actually quite a funny guy . . ."

"Stop it. I need to think."

"You think too much. That's your trouble. Just stop thinking." Frank breaks off midclick. "Oh. Shit. I don't know what I just did. Did you see what I did?"

"No."

"I think I deleted a document. Oops." He clicks madly. "Come on, you bastard—undo. Hey, don't tell Dad we did this, will you? Because if I've lost anything, he is going to go *insane*—"

Frank says something else, but I walk out, not even hearing him. My head is a whirl and my heart's thumping and I feel surreal.

Apologize. I can't imagine Izzy apologizing. I can't imagine Izzy saying a lot. She was never the main one. She sort of hung back and agreed and went along with Tasha. Well, let's face it, everyone in my class went along with Tasha. Because if *I* was the victim, then *they* weren't. Even Natalie stopped standing up for me—

No. Let's not go there anymore. Natalie was freaked out. I've made my peace with Natalie. It's all good.

Tasha is the one who's really scary. She's the one who makes my flesh crawl. She's bright and smart and motivated and pretty in that strong-jawed athletic way. All the teachers loved her. They *loved* her. You know, till they found out the truth and everything.

I've had a long time to think about this. And I've decided she did it for fun. You know. Because she *could*.

My theory is that Tasha will win awards one day. She'll

be some top advertising creative, selling a message to the public and getting everyone to believe it and doing it in a relentless, unremitting, really inspired way. She'll be one of those advertisers who trick you so you don't even realize you're being advertised to, you just give in and start to operate the way she wants you to. She'll use other people then discard them. Everyone she smiles at will fall under her spell and join the team. The people who hate her will feel totally used and wretched, but who cares about them?

The *real* truth, which by the way no grown-up would ever admit to, is that probably the whole experience will do her great in life. It was like, the most put-together project you could imagine. It was innovative. It was sustained. If it had been a GCSE project: *Torment Audrey Turner using a variety of imaginative methods*, she would have got A+ highly commended.

I mean yes, she got excluded in the end. But small detail, right?

In the end, I can't rest till I've had it out. So I march downstairs, way past eleven, when I should be asleep, and catch Mum and Dad in the kitchen making herbal teas.

"Mum, I read your email and I think I should go and see Izzy," I say.

There. Done.

So that was a no from Mum. And from Dad.

Mum got pretty mad. I mean, she was mad with Mrs. Lawton, she kept saying, but it sounded like she was more mad with me, from the way she kept coming back to the same topics.

I do appreciate that reading private emails is beyond the pale.

I do appreciate that Mum and Dad are juggling some big issues, and they can't do that if they're constantly afraid I'm going to hack into their email account all the time.

Do I want to turn into a household with locked doors? (No.)

Do I want to live in a family with no trust? (No.)

Wait a minute, was this Frank? Did Frank help you? (Silence.)

Mum's nostrils were white and her forehead veins were throbbing, and Dad looked grave, seriously grave, like he hasn't looked for a while, and they were both one hundred percent adamant that seeing Izzy was a nonstarter.

"You're *fragile*, Audrey," Mum kept saying. "You're like a piece of china that's just been mended."

She pinched that from Dr. Sarah.

Does Mum talk to Dr. Sarah behind my back? This has never occurred to me before. But then, I can clearly be quite slow off the mark.

"Sweetheart, I know you think it'll be a cathartic experience and you'll say your piece and everyone will come away the wiser," says Dad. "But in real life, that doesn't happen. I've confronted enough assholes in my time. They never realize they're assholes. Not once. Whatever you say." He turns to Mum. "Remember Ian? My first boss? Now, he was an asshole. Always was, always will be."

"I'm not planning to say a piece," I point out. "She's the one who wanted to apologise."

"She says," mutters Mum darkly. "She *says*."

"Tell us why you want to do it," says Dad. "Explain."

"Do you want to hear her say sorry?" says Mum. "We could tell her she has to write a letter."

"It's not that." I shake my head impatiently, trying to shift my thoughts into making sense. The trouble is, I can't explain. I don't know why I want to do it. Except maybe to prove something. But to who? Myself? Izzy?

Dr. Sarah isn't wild about hearing about Izzy or Tasha or any of them. She's all, like, "Audrey, you aren't validated by other people," and, "You're not responsible for other people's emotions" and "This Tasha sounds very tedious, let's move off the topic."

She even gave me a book about unhealthy relationships. (I

almost laughed out loud. Could you *get* any more unhealthy than the relationship between me and Tasha?) It was about how you have to be strong to break free from abuse and not constantly measure yourself against toxic people but stand strong and distinct like a healthy tree. Not some stunted, falling-over, codependent victim tree. Or whatever.

It's all very well. But Izzy and Tasha and all of them are still in my mind all the time. They have not checked out of the building. Maybe they never will.

"If I don't do it, it'll always be a question," I say at last. "It'll bug me my whole life. *Could* I have done it? *Would* it have changed things?"

Mum and Dad don't look convinced.

"You could say that about anything," says Mum. "*Could* you skydive off the Empire State Building? Well, maybe."

"Life's too short," says Dad firmly. "Move on."

"I'm *trying* to move on. This is part of moving on!"

But as I look from face to face I know I'm never going to persuade them. Never, whatever I say.

◆ ◆ ◆

So I go to Frank. Who also thinks it's a bad idea, but the difference is, after we've discussed it for about five minutes, he shrugs and says, "Your life."

Dad's changed his email password, but Frank soon finds it on his BlackBerry on a memo called New Password (poor Dad; he really shouldn't leave his BlackBerry lying around), and we get into the account. I was planning to write the email myself, but Frank takes over, and honestly, he sounds just like Dad.

"You've been reading too many of Dad's emails," I say in awe as I read his words. "This is amazing!"

"Piece of piss," says Frank, but I can tell he's pleased. And he should be. The email is totally a work of art. It goes like this:

Dear Mrs. Lawton

Please forgive my wife and me for our intemperate outburst of yesterday. As you can imagine, we were shocked at being contacted by you and perhaps reacted too quickly.

On reflection, Audrey would very much like to meet with Izzy and hear what she has to say. Could we suggest 3:00 p.m. next Tuesday, in Starbucks.

Please do not reply to this email, as my machine is playing up. Please text this number to confirm: 079986 435619.

With best wishes,
Chris Turner

That's my new mobile number. After we've sent the email, Frank deletes the email and then deletes it again out of Trash, and I think we're safe.

And then all of a sudden I feel this lurch of fright. What am I doing? Shit, what am I *doing*? My heart starts racing, and I can feel my hands twisting up into knots.

"Will you come with me? Please?" I say before I can stop myself, and Frank turns to give me a long look. I dodge it, turning my head, but then sneak a glance back. He's looking really anxious, like it's suddenly hit him too, what we've done.

"Aud, are you sure you want to do this?"

"Yes. Yes." I nod, over and over, as though to convince myself. "*Yes*. I'm going to do it. I just need a bit of moral support. If you come with me. And Linus."

"The three musketeers."

"Something like that."

"Have you told Linus?"

"No, but I'm meeting him later at the park. I'll tell him then."

As I get to the park, I have a really bad moment. One of the old, scary kinds. Everyone around looks like a robot out to get me, and the whole place is crackling with this air of dread and threat. My lizard brain is really not enjoying the experience; in fact, my lizard brain wants to crawl under a bush.

But I'm *not* crawling under bushes, I tell myself firmly. I'm *not* listening to any lizards. Even though I feel ill with fear and keep getting these weird, dizzy waves, I manage to stride into the park like a normal person, and spot Linus sitting on a bench. Seeing him anchors me a little. Seeing his orange-segment smile splitting his face, all wide and happy, just for me, feels like someone stroking my lizard brain and telling it to calm down, everything's fine.

(I haven't mentioned my lizard brain to Linus. I mean, there are some things you tell a boyfriend and there are some things you totally keep to yourself; otherwise you sound like a nutter.)

"Hey, Rhubarb."

"Hey, Orange Slice." I touch his hand and we brush mouths together.

"OK," says Linus, as soon as we part. "I have one. Go and ask that man if ducks are vegetarian." He points to an elderly man throwing bread at the ducks.

"Are ducks vegetarian?"

"Of course they're not, you dope. They eat worms. Go on." He pushes my shoulder and I get up with a grin. I'm pulsating with dread but I force myself to have a conversation with the guy about ducks. Then I return to the bench and tell Linus to go and ask a bunch of French tourists which country we're in.

Linus is a master. A *master.* He tells the French tourists in tones of consternation that he was aiming for Sweden, and must have gone astray, and they all start looking at maps and phones and saying *"Angleterre!* Eeengland!" to him and gesticulating at the red buses that pass the park every five seconds.

"Oh, *England,*" says Linus at last, and they all nod furiously and say *"D'accord! Grande Bretagne!* Eeengland!" and at last they head off, all still gabbling and looking back at him. They'll probably talk about him for the rest of their holiday.

"OK," says Linus as he returns to the bench. "Go and ask that guy if he sells coconut ice-cream." He nods at the ice-cream seller who has had his stall in the park every summer for as long as I can remember.

"He doesn't."

"I know. That's why you're asking."

"Too easy," I say proudly. "Think of another one."

"Can't be bothered," says Linus lazily. "Go and do ice-cream guy."

I head over to the stall and patiently wait my turn, and then say,

"Excuse me, do you sell coconut ice-cream?"

I know what he's going to say. I've asked for coconut ice-cream every year since I was about eight, but he never has it.

"I do today," says the ice-cream seller, his eyes twinkling. I stare at him stupidly as he reaches for his scoop.

"I'm sorry?"

"Coconut ice-cream for the young lady," he says with a flourish. "One-day special. Just for you."

"*What?*" I blink in disbelief as he scoops white ice-cream into a massive cone. "Is that coconut?"

"Just for you," he repeats, handing me the cone. "And a chocolate-chip for the young man," he adds, handing me a second cone. "All paid for."

"Coconut's my favourite flavour," I say, in a daze. "But you never have it."

"That's what he said. Your young man. Asked me to get it in special-like."

I swivel round, and Linus is watching, his smile wider than ever.

"Thanks," I say to the ice-cream seller. "I mean, *thanks.*"

As I reach Linus, I fling my arms round him without dropping either ice-cream and kiss him. "I can't believe you did that!" I hand him his cone and lick my own. It's nectar.

It's bliss. Coconut is the best flavour in the world. "Oh my *God*."

"Nice?"

"I love it. I *love* it."

"So do I," says Linus, licking his own cone. "You."

His words catch on my brain. *So do I. You.*

The park is a riot of sunshine and ducks quacking and children shrieking, but right now it's as though the whole world has shrunk to his face. His brown hair, his honest eyes, that crescent smile.

"What . . . do you mean?" I force the words out.

"What I said. I love it too," he says, not taking his eyes off mine.

"You said *you*."

"Well . . . maybe that's what I meant."

I love it. So do I. You.

The words are dancing round my mind like jigsaw pieces, fitting together this way and that way.

"What, exactly?" I have to say it.

"You know exactly." His eyes are smiling to match his orange-segment mouth. But they're grave too.

"Well . . . I love it too," I say, my throat tight. "You."

"Me."

"Yes." I swallow. "Yes."

We don't need to say any more. And I know I'll always remember this moment, right here, standing in the park with the ducks and the sunshine and his arms round me. His kiss tastes of chocolate-chip and I'm sure I taste of coconut.

Actually, those flavours go very well together. So.

◆ ◆ ◆

And it's only later that life disintegrates.

He doesn't understand. He won't understand. He's not just opposed to the plan, he's angry. Physically angry. He hits a tree, like it's the tree's fault.

"It's fucking nuts," he keeps saying, striding back and forth over the grass, glaring at the squirrels. "Bonkers."

"Look, Linus . . ." I try to explain. "I have to do this."

"Don't give me that bollocks!" he yells. "I thought your therapist banned those words? I thought the only thing you 'have to' do in life is obey the laws of physics? Didn't you learn anything? What about living in the present, not the past? What about that?"

I stare at him, silenced. He was listening more than I realized.

"You don't 'have to' do this," he continues, "you're *choosing* to do it. What if you have a relapse? What then?"

"Then . . ." I wipe my damp face. "I won't. I'll be fine. I'm *better*, in case you hadn't realized—"

"You're still wearing fucking dark glasses!" he explodes. "You're still practicing having three-line conversations with strangers! And now you want to face down some bitch bully girl? Why would you even give her the time of day? It's selfish."

"What?" I stare at him, reeling. *"Selfish?"*

"Yes, selfish! You know how many people have tried to help you? You know how many people are willing you to get better? And you pull a stunt like this, just because you 'have to'? This is dangerous, if you ask me. And who's going to pick up the pieces afterwards? Tell me that."

He's so righteously indignant, I feel a surge of fury. What does he know? What the *fuck* does he know about me?

"There won't be any 'pieces,'" I spit at him. "For God's sake, seeing one girl in Starbucks isn't *dangerous*. And anyway, it wasn't *what happened* that made me ill. That's a common mistake people make, *actually*. Stressful events don't make you ill, *actually*. It's the way your brain reacts to stressful events. So."

"OK, so how's your brain going to react to this stressful event?" he shoots back with equal ferocity. "Do a dance and sing 'Happy'?"

"It's going to react fine," I say savagely. "I'm *better*. And if by any chance it doesn't, don't worry, I won't expect you to pick up the pieces. In fact, you know, Linus, I'm sorry I've caused you so much trouble already. You'd better find someone else to hang out with. Someone who doesn't possess any dark glasses. Maybe Tasha, I've heard she's super-fun."

I'm scrambling to my feet, trying to keep my poise, which isn't easy when the landscape is looming at me and my head is singing loud protests.

"Audrey, stop."

"No. I'm going."

Tears are coursing down my face, but that's OK, because I'm keeping it twisted away from Linus.

"Well, I'm coming with you."

"Leave me alone," I say, wrenching my arm out of his grasp. "Leave me *alone*." And finally, after managing to ignore it all day, I surrender to my lizard brain. And I run.

Here's what I'm not supposed to do after a stressful event: Ruminate about it. Brood. Replay it over and over. Take responsibility for anyone else's emotions.

Here's what I've been doing ever since my fight with Linus: Ruminating about it. Brooding. Replaying it over and over. Taking responsibility for his fury (yet resenting it). Lurching between despair and indignation. Wanting to call him. Wanting to never call him again.

Why can't he *understand*? I thought he'd admire me. I thought he'd talk about Closure and Courage and say, "You're right, Audrey, this is something you have to do, however hard it is, and I'll be right behind you."

I've barely slept, the last two nights. It's like my mind is a cauldron, cooking away, throwing up noxious bubbles and fumes and fermenting itself into something quite weird. I feel light-headed and surreal and hyper. But kind of focused too. I'm going to do this, and it's going to be like a major turning point, and afterwards things will be different. I don't know how exactly, but they will. It's like, I'll have got over the hurdle or run through the finishing tape or whatever. I'll be free. Of something.

So in short, I'm a bit obsessed. But luckily Mum and Dad are too preoccupied with Frank to notice me right now. I'm way down under their radar. Basically, Mum found the Atari in Frank's room last night and it all kicked off again and now we're in Family Crisis Mode.

As I come down to breakfast, they're at it again.

"For the millionth time, it's *not* a computer," Frank is saying calmly. "It's an Atari console. You said no computers. I classify a computer as a machine which can process information in a number of ways, including word processing, email and Internet browsing. The Atari does none of these, therefore it's not a computer, therefore it wasn't a basic breach of trust." He shovels Shreddies into his mouth. "You need to tighten up your definitions. That's the problem. Not my Atari console."

I think Frank should be a lawyer one day. I mean, he's totally nailed the argument, not that Mum appreciates it.

"Do you hear this?" Mum is appealing to Dad, who looks like he wants to hide behind his newspaper. "The point is, Frank, we had an agreement. You do not play any kind of video games, end of. Do you *know* how damaging they are?"

"Jesus." Frank holds his head in his hands. "Mum, you're the one with a problem with computer games. You're becoming fixated."

"I'm not fixated!" She gives a scoffing laugh.

"You are! You can't think about anything else! Do you even *know* that I got ninety-five in my chemistry?"

"Ninety-five?" Mum is stopped in her tracks. "Really?"

"I told you yesterday, but you didn't even listen. You were all, *Atari! Evil! Get it out of the house!*"

Mum looks a bit chastened.

"Oh," she says at last. "Well . . . ninety-five! That's great! Well done!"

"Out of a thousand," says Frank, then adds, "Joke. *Joke.*"

He grins at me, and I try to smile back, though my stomach is churning. All I can think is: *Three o'clock. Three o'clock.*

We've stuck to the meeting place in Starbucks, even though the Lawtons have been constantly texting, wanting to change it to a "more conducive location" and offering their own house or a hotel suite or a room at Izzy's counsellor's office. Yeah, right.

Frank has been in charge of all the correspondence. He's brilliant. He's batted away all their suggestions in a way that could totally be Dad, and refused to give them an alternative email address, which they keep asking for, and texted in exactly Dad's style.

It's actually quite funny. I mean, they have no idea it's just us, two kids. They think Dad and Mum are coming. They think this is a big family meeting. They hope it will be "cathartic for all," according to their last text.

As for me, I can't believe I'm going to see Izzy again. It's going to happen. The big showdown. I feel like I'm a spring that is slowly coiling up and up, tensing, waiting . . .

Only seven hours to go.

And then suddenly it's seven minutes to go and I truly feel sick. My head is pounding, not with a headache, but with a kind of impending, heightened sense of reality. The street seems brighter than normal, somehow. Noisier. Rawer.

Frank's bunked off school early, which is OK because exams are over, so all they do in lessons is watch "educational" DVDs. He's walking along with me, chatting about what happened in assembly this morning when someone brought their pet rat in and let it go. I half want to snap, "Shut up! Let me think!" and I'm half grateful for the distraction.

I'm wearing jeans and a black T-shirt and black trainers. Serious clothes. I have no idea what Izzy will wear. She was never a particularly cool dresser; that was Tasha. I even half wonder if I'll recognize her. I mean, it wasn't that long ago, but it feels a whole lifetime.

But of course I do recognize her, instantly. I see them through the glass before they see us. The mother, the father, both looking anxious, but doing that fake smile thing. And her. Izzy. She's in some childlike T-shirt with pink ribbon edging, and a pretty skirt. What's *that* all about? I want to laugh. But . . . I can't.

I can't smile either. It's like all my powers are slipping away, one by one.

As I step inside the coffee shop, I know I can't speak. My insides have turned hollow. Just like that, in an instant. All the inner strength I've been building up, the tensed-up spring, the fighting talk . . . it's all disappeared.

I feel small and vulnerable.

No, not small. I'm taller than her. I still have that. I'm tall.

But vulnerable. And speechless. And now they're all looking our way. I squeeze Frank's hand in silent desperation and he seems to get the message.

"Hello," he says briskly, heading towards their table. "Let me introduce myself. Frank Turner. You must be the Lawtons."

He holds out his hand but no-one takes it. Both of Izzy's parents are looking him up and down in bewilderment.

"Audrey, we were expecting your parents," says Mrs. Lawton.

"They were unavoidably detained," says Frank without blinking. "I am the family representative."

"But—" Mrs. Lawton looks flustered. "I really think your parents should— We understood this would be a family meeting."

"I am the Turner family representative," Frank repeats adamantly. He pulls out a chair and we sit down opposite them. The Lawtons look at each other anxiously and make little mouthing gestures and raised-eyebrow signals, but after a while they quieten down and it's clear that the conversation about parents is over.

"We bought some bottles of water," says Mrs. Lawton, "but we can get some teas, coffees, whatever?"

"Water is fine," says Frank. "Let's get to the point, shall we? Izzy wants to apologise to Audrey, yes?"

"Let's put this in context," says Mr. Lawton heavily. "We, like you, have gone through some pretty hellish months.

We've asked ourselves why, over and over. Izzy has asked herself why too. Haven't you, darling?" He looks gravely at Izzy. "How could such a thing happen? And, in a way, what *did* happen and who, in actual fact, was at fault?"

He presses a hand to Izzy's, and I look at her properly for the first time. God, she looks different. She looks like an eleven-year-old, I suddenly realize. It's kind of *disturbing*. Her hair is in a ponytail with a little-girl bobble, and there's the infantile ribbony T-shirt going on, and she's looking up at her father with huge baby eyes. She's wearing some kind of sickly strawberry lip gloss. I can smell it from here.

She hasn't given me a single glance this whole time. And her parents haven't made her. If I were them, that's the first thing I would do. Make her look at me. Make her *see* me.

"Izzy has been through a pretty tough journey." Mr. Lawton continues on what is clearly a prepared speech. "As you know, she's homeschooled for now, and she's undergone a fairly rigorous program of counselling."

Snap, I think.

"But she's finding it hard to move on." Mr. Lawton clutches Izzy's hand, and she looks imploringly up at him. "Aren't you, darling? She unfortunately suffers from clinical depression."

He says it like it's a trump card. What, are we supposed to applaud? Tell him how sorry we are, *wow, depression, that must be horrible*?

"So what?" says Frank scathingly. "So's Audrey." He addresses Izzy directly. "I know what you did to my sister. I'd be depressed if I were you too."

Both Lawtons inhale sharply and Mr. Lawton puts a hand to his head.

"I was hoping for a more *constructive* approach to the meeting," he says. "Perhaps we could keep the insults to ourselves?"

"That's not an insult!" says Frank. "It's the truth! And I thought Izzy was going to apologise? Where's the apology?" He pokes Izzy's arm and she withdraws it with a gasp.

"Izzy has been working with her team," says Mr. Lawton. "She's written a piece which she would like to deliver to Audrey." He pats Izzy on the shoulder. "Izzy devised this in one of her poetry workshops."

Poetry? *Poetry?*

I hear Frank snort and both Lawtons look at him with dislike.

"This will be hard for Izzy," says Mrs. Lawton coldly. "She is very fragile."

"As we all are," says Mr. Lawton, nodding at me and making a face at his wife.

"Yes, of course," says Mrs. Lawton, but she doesn't sound convinced. "So we ask you to listen to her piece in silence, without comment. Then we can move into the discussion phase of the meeting."

There's silence as Izzy unfurls a wad of A4 pages. She still hasn't looked at me properly. *Still.*

"You can do it, Izzy," whispers her mother. "Be brave." Her father pats her hand and I see Frank make a barf gesture.

" 'When the darkness came,' " says Izzy in a trembling voice. "By Isobel Lawton. 'It came on me, the darkness. I followed when I should not. I acted when I should not. And now I look back and I know that my life is a twisted knot . . .' "

OK, if they paid good money for this poetry workshop, they were done.

As I listen to the words, I'm waiting for some strong, visceral reaction. I'm waiting for some part of me to rise up and hate her or attack her or something. I'm waiting for the big moment, the confrontation. But it's not coming. I can't get traction. I can't *feel* it.

Since the moment I stepped through the door, this hasn't been what I thought it would be. I'm not the warrior I imagined. I'm hollow and vulnerable and kind of *lesser.* I'm not winning any battle, sitting here, silently clutching the table, unable to speak, just thinking my own rapid, restless thoughts.

But more than that—there isn't even any battle to have, is there? The Lawtons aren't interested in me. I could say what I like—they wouldn't listen. They're playing out their little story in which Izzy apologises and she's the hero and I'm the bit part. And I'm letting them do it. Why am I letting them do it?

I feel a sudden wave of revulsion as I survey Izzy's bowed head.

She won't look at me, will she? She can't. Because I might pop the bubble.

I mean, I guess that's one way to go. Slip back into being eleven years old, wear ponytails, and get homeschooled and let your parents take over and tell you everything's OK, you weren't *really* a bullying monster, my sweetheart. It was the nasty people who didn't understand you. But if you write a poem, everything will be OK.

Out of nowhere, Linus's voice comes into my head: *Why would you even give her the time of day?*

Why would I? Why *am* I giving her the time of day? What am I doing here?

" '. . . but bad forces come from every direction, no affection, just affliction . . .' "

Izzy is still droning on in what seems to have become a tragically bad rap. She's got another A4 page to go, I notice. It's definitely time to leave.

I squeeze Frank's hand and look at the door. He raises his eyebrows and I nod firmly. I even make a small, inarticulate sound.

"Yes, we have to go now," says Frank, cutting across Izzy. "Thanks for the water."

"Go?"

The Lawtons look poleaxed.

"But Izzy hasn't finished reading."

"We haven't had any discussion."

"We've only just begun the meeting!"

"That's right," says Frank cheerfully as we both get to our feet. "OK, Aud?"

"You can't leave before Izzy has even finished her piece!" Mrs. Lawton sounds quite shirty. "I'm sorry, what kind of behaviour is this?"

And then I finally find my voice. "You want to talk about *behaviour*?" I say quietly.

It's like a magic charm. Everyone else is silenced. Paralysed.

There's an odd hush around the place—it feels like the whole of Starbucks might have picked up on our vibe, just for a second. Mr. Lawton's face has kind of crumpled. It's as if reality has pushed its way through his soap bubble of denial, just for a second, and he's been forced to see exactly who I am. I'm the one they did all those things to.

Yes, those things. The ones they did. And said. And wrote. Your daughter in her ponytail. That's right.

I don't look at Izzy. Why would I expend the energy that swiveling my eyeballs in her direction would require? Why would I expend even one microjoule of energy on Izzy?

And then we're walking out, Frank and I, not looking back, not talking about it, not wasting a second more of our lives on that load of shitty, shitty *crap.*

And I should feel high now. Shouldn't I? I mean, I think I won. Didn't I?

Only now it's all over, I just feel kind of empty. Frank's sole comment as we walked back was "What a bunch of weirdos." Then he told me he was heading back to school for tech club and when I gave him a big hug and muttered "Thanks, I don't know how I can repay you," into his shoulder, he said "OK, well, I get to choose *both* pizza toppings on Friday night. OK?"

And now it's seven o'clock and I'm on my own. Mum and Dad are out at their salsa class. They have no idea. I mean, how weird is that? I've actually *met up with Izzy* and they don't know.

I've texted Linus and told him about it. I've said I'm sorry I blew up at him. I've said he was right, I should never have gone and I miss him and I want to see him so, so much.

I want to go back to how we were. I want him to give me another crazy challenge. I want to forget I ever went to see Izzy.

I mean, I think we were both right. I was right because I didn't relapse and there aren't any pieces to pick up. And Linus was right because I shouldn't have given her the time of day in the first place. So. And when he texts back, I'll ask him round and maybe we'll get back to that *other* conversation we were having in the park.

◆ ◆ ◆

That was two hours ago and he still hasn't texted back. I've checked my phone signal like a million times and it's fine. Anyway. Maybe he's busy or whatever.

◆ ◆ ◆

Except by ten o'clock he still hasn't texted back. And he *always* texts back. Always within the hour. He finds a way. He's texted me from lessons, from his family supper, wherever. He doesn't not text. But right now he's not texting.

◆ ◆ ◆

It's eleven. He's not texting.

◆ ◆ ◆

It's midnight. No text.

◆ ◆ ◆

And now it's one o'clock, and I don't know what to do. I can't sleep. I can't even lie down. I officially "went to bed" three hours ago but I haven't touched the covers. I'm pacing around my room, trying to calm my whirling thoughts, but they're like a hurricane.

I've wrecked everything with Linus. He's never texting. It's over. He was right, I was selfish. I should never have gone to that stupid meeting. Why did I do it? Why? I always do stupid things. I'm such a stupid, *idiot* failure, and now I've spoiled the only good thing I had in my life, and he hates me and there's nothing I can do about it. The whole thing's over. And it's all my fault, my stupid, *stupid* fault . . .

My thoughts are speeding up and my pace is speeding up too, and I'm pulling at my arms, pulling at the flesh of my forearms, trying to . . . I don't know. I don't understand it. I glance in the mirror and flinch at my own wild stare. I can feel a weird sparking all over my body, like I'm more alive than I should be, like my body is *overloaded* with life force. Can you have too much life stuffed into one body? Because that's what this feels like. And everything's too fast. My heart, my thoughts, my feet, my clawing arms . . .

Maybe I should take something. The thought hits me like a very sensible person talking in my ear. Yes. Of course. I have things I could take. I have lots of things.

I rootle around in my box full of magic tricks, dropping bottles and packets on the floor in my haste. OK, a Clonazepam. Maybe two. Maybe three. I swallow them, and wait for everything to calm down. But my mind is still screaming, round and round like a motor race, and I can't stand it. I can't stand myself. I *have* to escape . . .

When suddenly another brilliant idea hits me. I'll go for a walk. I'll burn off all this energy. The fresh air will do me a power of good. And I'll come back and sleep it off and, like they say, things will be better in the morning.

MY SERENE AND LOVING FAMILY—FILM TRANSCRIPT

INTERIOR. 5 ROSEWOOD CLOSE. DAY.

The camera wobbles as someone stabilises it on a high
surface. As this person backs away we see it is Frank,
in the sitting room. He stares into the camera with
deeply worried eyes.

> **FRANK**
> Is this working? OK. Hello. I'm Frank
> Turner and this is my video diary.
> My sister Audrey is missing. It's a
> nightmare. We woke up this morning
> and there she wasn't. Mum and Dad are
> just . . . (He swallows.) We've looked
> everywhere, and we've phoned everyone.
> Mum and Dad called the police, like,
> *that instant*. And the police are great,
> they're really calm. But . . .

He shuts his eyes briefly.

> **FRANK**
> I still don't believe this is happening.

He's silent a while, his eyes hollow.

> **FRANK**
> They blame me. Which is . . .

He exhales miserably.

> **FRANK**
> Anyway. We're going out again in a
> minute, to look again. I dunno where—I

                    mean, we've looked everywhere. All the
                    little side alleys, maybe? But Mum said
                    I should have some food first. Like
                    anyone wants to *eat*.

He gives another heavy sigh.

                             FRANK
                    Anyway. I told them what we did
                    yesterday. I had to. Audrey, if you're
                    watching this, I *had* to.

Long pause.

                             FRANK
                    Audrey, please come home and be
                    watching this.

The doorbell rings and he jumps a mile.

                             FRANK
                    Wait a sec.

He runs out of the room. A few seconds elapse, then he
returns, slack-shouldered, accompanied by Linus.

                             FRANK
                         (into camera)
                    It wasn't her. It was Linus.

                             LINUS
                         (to Frank)
                    Sorry.

He looks awkwardly into the camera.

                             LINUS
                    Sorry.

Mum comes striding into the room, her face drawn, her
eyes burning with purpose, her manner hyper.

                    MUM
          Frank, we're going through her things,
          and I need to know—

She sees Linus and stops dead, full of hostility.

                    MUM
          You. What are you doing here?

Linus is shocked by her aggression.

                    LINUS
          Me? I just—Frank told me about Audrey,
          so—

                    MUM
          Do you know where she is?

                    LINUS
          No! Of course not! I would have said!

He gulps nervously at Mum's manner but carries on.

                    LINUS
          Frank said you wanted to know who
          she'd been texting? Well, she sent me
          this text yesterday, but it only came
          through just now. I had no idea she'd
          texted.

He holds out his phone.

                    LINUS
          I mean, I don't know if it helps.

Mum scans the phone, getting agitated as she does so.

                              MUM
                          (to Linus)
          So you knew about this meeting with the
          Lawtons too. Was it your idea?

                             LINUS
          No!

                              MUM
          But you've been telling her to "do
          crazy challenges," apparently.

She taps the phone.

                              MUM
          She says she wants you to give her
          another "crazy challenge."

                             LINUS
                          (alarmed)
          Not that kind of crazy challenge. Just
          talking to people in Starbucks and
          stuff.

Mum doesn't seem to hear him.

                              MUM
          Was this, leaving home in the middle of
          the night, was this one of your "crazy
          challenges," Linus?

                             LINUS
          No! How could you even—

He appeals to Frank.

                             LINUS
          Would I do that?

                    FRANK
        Mum, you're out of line.

Mum rounds on Linus.

                    MUM
        All I know is, she was on an even
        keel till she met you. And now she's
        missing.

                    LINUS
        That is so unfair.

He's having trouble holding it together.

                    LINUS
        So unfair. I have to go. Let me know
        if I can help.

As Linus leaves, Frank turns furiously on Mum.

                    FRANK
        How could you blame Linus? Of all
        people. This house is so fucked up.

Mum erupts in a flood of sudden anguish.

                    MUM
        She's missing, Frank! Don't you
        understand, she's *missing*. I have to
        try everything, I have to consider
        everything, every possibility—

She breaks off as Dad appears, breathless, holding his
mobile.

                    DAD
        They've found her. In the park.
        Asleep. She was hidden away,

behind a—

We must have missed her—

He can barely form his words.

                              DAD

They've got her.

The weird thing is, I lost my sunglasses that night and I didn't even notice until Dad suddenly said, "Audrey! You're not wearing your dark glasses!"

And I wasn't. My eyes were bare. After all those months. And it took Dad to point it out to me.

We were in the police waiting room at the time, and the nice police woman, Sinead, got the wrong end of the stick and thought we were complaining and that we'd lost a pair of dark glasses on the premises. It took a while for us to explain that I didn't *want* them back.

And I don't. I'm good the way I am. The world seems lighter, although I don't know if that's because of the dark glasses or because I'm back on my meds. For now. Dr. Sarah gave me this whole great lecture about the dangers of coming off meds without supervision and how it can cause dizziness (check) and a racing heart (check) and loads of other symptoms and I must promise never to do it again. Which I did.

The stuff she gave me kind of knocked me out, so I've been sleeping a lot these last two days, but everyone's come into my room to see me, like, all the time. To make sure I'm still here, I guess.

Dad has told me about the new song he's writing, and Frank has shown me endless YouTube clips of knife skills (which he is getting very boring about) and Felix has told me he cut the hair of his friend Ben at school and Ben cried. This is apparently true, according to Dad, but Felix maintains that Ben cried "because he was *happy.*"

Mum's been in to see me the most. She sat on my bed all afternoon and we watched *Little Women,* which is like the perfect movie to watch with your mum when you're in bed, feeling a bit weird. (The old one with Elizabeth Taylor, in case you're wondering.)

While we were watching, we decorated these handbags we'd made out of felt yesterday. This is Mum's new thing: she buys little craft projects and we make them together. Neither of us is very good at it, but . . . you know. It's nice. It's relaxing. It's not *about* anything. And Mum just sits on my bed, hanging out, not looking anxiously around the room, not trying to get clues to my thoughts. I don't think she needs clues anymore. She knows. Or at least, she knows enough.

It was while I was trying to glue an appliqué star onto the front of my bag that I said, "Mum, why don't you go back to work?"

Mum kind of stiffened. She carefully looped a piece of ribbon into a bow and stapled it before looking up and saying, "Work?"

"Yes, work. You haven't been for ages. Not since ..." I trailed off.

"Well, it's been difficult." Mum gave a short laugh.

"I know. But you're brilliant at your job. And you win prizes and you wear great jackets ..."

Mum threw back her head and laughed again. "Darling, you don't go to work just to wear great jackets." She thinks for a moment. "Well, most of the time you don't."

"You're staying at home because of me, aren't you?" I persisted.

"Sweetheart ..." Mum sighed. "I love being here with you. I wouldn't want to be anywhere else."

"I know."

There was silence and we watched as Jo turned down Laurie's proposal, which, every time I watch it, I wish she would say yes.

"But still, I think you should go back to work," I said. "You're all shiny when you're at work."

"*Shiny?*" Mum seemed a bit taken aback.

"Shiny. Like, super-mum."

Mum looked incredibly touched. She blinked a few times and threaded another ribbon through the bow, and then said,

"It's not as simple as that, Audrey. I might have to travel, there are long hours, you're starting a new school ..."

"So we'll make it work," I said, as robustly as I could. "Mum, there's no point me getting better if things don't get better for all of us. I mean, we've *all* had a bad time, haven't we?"

I'd been thinking about that all morning. About how it would be easy for me to get better and spring happily

265

through the door, and leave Mum and Dad and Frank and Felix behind. But it shouldn't be like that. We were all affected by what happened. We should all spring happily out of the door *together.*

Well, you know. Maybe Frank could slouch happily.

We watched for a while more in silence. Then Mum said, as though she was carrying on the same conversation,

"Dr. Sarah told me why you ditched your meds. You wanted to have a straight graph?"

My heart kind of sank. I had *really* not wanted to get onto the subject of meds. But I might have known it would come up.

"I wanted to be better," I mumbled, feeling hot. "You know. Properly, one hundred percent better. No meds, nothing."

"You *are* better." Mum put my face between her hands, just like she used to when I was a little girl. "Sweetheart, you're so much better every week. I mean, you're a different girl. You're ninety percent there. Ninety-five percent. You must be able to see that."

"But I'm sick of this bloody jagged graph," I said in frustration. "You know, two steps up, one step down. It's so *painful.* It's so *slow.* It's like this endless game of snakes and ladders."

And Mum just looked at me as if she wanted to laugh or maybe cry, and she said, "But, Audrey, that's what life is. We're all on a jagged graph. I know I am. Up a bit, down a bit. That's life."

And then Jo met Professor Bhaer, so we had to watch that bit.

And then Beth died. So I guess the March sisters were on their own jagged graph too.

That night I come downstairs for a cup of hot chocolate and hear Dad saying, "Anne, I've ordered Frank a new laptop. There. I've said it. It's done."

Wow.

I creep forward and peer through the open door to see Mum almost drop her mug.

"A new *laptop*?"

"Secondhand. Excellent price. I went to Paul Taylor, he has some good deals—" Dad breaks off at Mum's expression. "Anne, OK. I know what we said. I *know*. But I can't cope with the tension in this house anymore. And Frank's right, he does need the Internet for his schoolwork, and he can hack into my emails, as we now know . . ."

"I can't believe you just went and did it."

Mum is shaking her head, but she doesn't sound quite as shrieky as I was expecting. In fact, she seems almost calm.

It's eerie. I'm not sure I like Mum calm. She's better all mad and voluble.

"Is it *so* bad for Frank to play computer games once in a while?" ventures Dad.

"Oh, I don't know, Chris." Mum rubs her face. "I don't know anymore. About anything."

"Well, nor do I." He pulls her in for a hug. "Anyway, I've got him a laptop."

"OK." Mum kind of subsides onto Dad and I can see how tired out she is. Frank said he's never seen Mum like she was when I was missing. She was kind of grey, he said. And her eyes were flat inside, like their battery had died.

I'll never get over doing that to them. But I'm not brooding. I've talked to Dr. Sarah about it and we've agreed that the best way I can make it up to them is to stay well. Stay on my meds. Think healthful thoughts.

"You remember that Christmas when they got ill?" Mum says presently. "The year they were about two and three? Remember? And got poo all over their Christmas stockings, and it was *everywhere*, and we said, 'It has to get easier than this'?"

"I remember."

"We were cleaning it all up and we kept saying to each other, 'When they get older, it'll get easier.' Remember?"

"I do." Dad looks fondly at her.

"Well, bring back the poo." Mum begins to laugh, a bit hysterically. "I would do anything for a bit of poo right now."

"I dream of poo," says Dad firmly, and Mum laughs even more, till she's wiping tears from her eyes.

And I back away, without making a sound. I'll get my hot chocolate later.

And so the only piece left in the jigsaw is Linus. But it's a big piece.

Frank just showed me the footage of Mum laying into Linus in the sitting room and I stared in total disbelief. First, I couldn't believe Mum could blame Linus for anything, Second, I couldn't believe he'd only just got my text. Third, I couldn't believe he'd come over to see me.

So he hadn't given up on me. He didn't hate me. I hadn't spoiled everything. I'd been wrong on pretty much everything. As I watched it for the second time I felt pretty sheepish, and I could tell Mum felt even worse.

"I *don't* sound like that," she kept saying in horror. "I *didn't* say that. Did I?"

"You totally sound like that," said Frank. "You sound worse, actually. The camera was flattering."

He was rubbing it in. She doesn't sound *quite* as shrill as that in real life.

"So, I need to apologise to Linus." She sighs.

"So do I," I say quickly.

"So do I," says Frank glumly.

"What?" Mum and I swivel to look at him.

"We had a fight. About *LOC*. He was talking about the tournament and I got . . . well, jealous, I suppose."

Frank looks like an overgrown schoolboy. He's got ink on his hands and is staring miserably at his knees. He doesn't know about the laptop yet, and I would love to whisper it in his ear to cheer him up, but I've had enough of going behind my parents' backs. For now.

"So." Mum is back into her brisk mode again. "We all need to apologise to Linus."

"Mum, that's all very well," I say in a flat tone. "But it's too late. Linus's parents are emigrating. He's at the airport right now. We've missed our chance."

"What?" Mum looks up as though scalded.

"We could make the airport." Dad looks alertly at his watch. "Which airport? Anne, we'll take your car."

"Which flight?" demands Mum. "Audrey, which flight?"

What are my parents *like*? They've watched too many Richard Curtis films, that's their trouble. They've gone soft in the head.

"He's not at the bloody *airport!*" I expostulate. "I said that as a *joke*. Don't you think you'd know if Linus was emigrating?"

"Oh." Mum subsides, looking highly embarrassed. "OK. I just got carried away for a moment. What shall we do, then?"

"Invite him to Starbucks," I say after a moment's thought. "It needs to be at Starbucks. Frank, you text him."

It's actually pretty funny. When Linus arrives at Starbucks, we're all sitting there at one big table, the whole family, waiting for him. He looks totally unnerved, and for a moment I think he's going to run away, but you know, Linus isn't a runner-awayer. After about five seconds he comes forward resolutely and looks at us all in turn, especially Mum. And last of all me.

It takes him about thirty seconds to realize.

"Your glasses!"

"I know." I can't help beaming.

"When—?"

"Dunno. They just fell off. And . . . here I am."

"So, Linus," says Mum. "We would all like to apologise to you. Frank?"

"Sorry I got ratty, mate," says Frank, turning red.

"Oh." Linus seems embarrassed. "Er . . . that's OK."

They bang fists together then Frank turns to Mum.

"Mum, your turn."

"OK." Mum clears her throat. "Linus, I'm very sorry I took my worries and fears out on you. I got completely the wrong end of the stick. I know how good you've been for Audrey and I can only apologise."

"Right. Um." Linus looks even more embarrassed. "Listen, you don't have to do this," he says, looking around the family. "I know you were all stressed."

"We want to." Mum's voice gives a sudden waver. "Linus, we're all very fond of you. And I should *not* have shouted at you. It was a bad time, and I really am sorry."

"Sorry!" chimes in Felix, who has been chomping on

shortbread biscuits all this time. "We have to say sorry to Linus. Sorry, Linus." He beams. "Sorry, Linus."

"Felix, you're fine," says Linus.

I can see Felix gazing at Linus, his dandelion clock head on one side, as though trying to work out what we're all doing here.

"Did Mummy cut your hair?" he says, as though he's cracked it. "Did you cry? Ben cried because he was *happy*."

"Er, no, Felix, no-one cut my hair," says Linus, looking baffled.

"Ben cried because he was *happy*," reiterates Felix.

"So that's me," says Mum. "Chris? Your turn?" She turns to Dad, who looks a little startled. I'm not sure he realized this was a go-round-the-table apology.

"Er . . . hear, hear," he says. "What she said." He waves towards Mum. "Count me in on that. Understood?"

"Understood," says Linus with a little smile.

"And, Linus, we'd like to give you a little present to make amends," says Mum. "A little gift. Maybe a theatre outing . . . or a theme park? You choose."

"I can choose anything?" Linus looks secretively from Mum to Dad. "Anything I want?"

"Well, within reason! Nothing *too* expensive . . ."

"This wouldn't be expensive, what I'm thinking of."

"It sounds great!" says Dad at once, and Mum frowns at him.

"I want to play in the *LOC* qualifiers with Frank," says Linus. "That's what I want more than anything."

"Oh." Mum stares at him, discomfited. "Really?"

"You're in a team already," says Frank gruffly. I can tell he's super-touched from the way he won't even look at Linus.

"I want to play in your team. They've got a reserve. They don't need me."

"But we haven't got a team!" says Frank, and there's a sudden depth of misery to his voice. "I haven't got a computer, we don't have a team—"

"Yet," chimes in Dad, bubbling over. "Yet." He grins madly at Frank. "Yet."

"What?" Frank stares blankly at him.

"You haven't got a computer *yet.*" Dad gives one of his stage winks. "Just look out for a big brown box, is all I'm saying. But no more hacking my emails."

"What?" Frank looks almost heady with hope. "Seriously?"

"*If* you follow our rules and don't make a fuss when we tell you to stop playing," says Mum. "If there's any trouble, it's going out of the window." She gives a satisfied little grin. "You know I'll do it. You know I want to."

"Anything!" Frank seems almost beyond speechless. "I'll do anything!"

"So you can play in your game," says Dad, who looks almost as fired up by this as Frank. "I was reading a piece about it in the *Sunday Times* magazine. I mean, this *LOC* is a big business, isn't it?"

"Yes!" says Frank, as if to say *Finally!* "In Korea it's an official spectator sport! And they have scholarships for it in the States. Actual scholarships."

"You should read the piece, Anne," says Dad. "What's the prize pot, six million dollars?" He grins at Frank. "So, are you going to win that?"

"We don't have a team." Frank suddenly deflates. "We'll never get a team together. It's, like, a week away."

"Ollie could play," suggests Linus. "He's not bad, for a twelve-year-old."

"I could play," I offer, on impulse. "You know, if you want me to."

"You?" says Frank derisively. "You're crap."

"Well, I can practice, can't I?"

"Exactly!" says Mum. "She can practice. So, that's sorted." She glances at her watch, then at Linus and me. "And now we'll leave you two alone, for Audrey to ... Well, for you to ..." She pauses. "Anyway. You don't want us hanging around embarrassing you!"

OK, the thing is, no-one was embarrassed till she said the word *embarrassed*. As it is, Linus and I wait in awkward silence while they all get up and Felix drops his biscuit and wants another one, and Dad starts looking for his BlackBerry and Mum tells him he didn't have it, and honestly, I love them to bits, but could my family be *any* more annoying?

I wait until they've well and truly left and the glass door has closed behind them. And then I turn properly to Linus and look at him.

"Welcome to my eyes," I say softly. "What do you think?"

"I like them." He smiles. "I love them."

We're just looking and looking at each other. And I can feel something new between us, something even more intimate than anything we've done. Eye to eye. It's the most powerful connection in the world.

"Linus, I'm sorry," I say at last, wrenching my gaze away. "I should have listened, you were right—"

"Stop." He plants his hand on mine. "You've said it. I've said it. Enough."

He has a point. We've sent about five zillion texts to each other since I came back. (Only Mum isn't supposed to know how many, because I was "resting.")

"So . . . are we OK?"

"Well, that depends," says Linus, and I feel a lurch of fear in spite of myself.

"On what?"

Linus looks at me thoughtfully for a moment. "On whether you can ask that blond woman three tables away directions to the circus."

I start laughing in a way I haven't for ages. "The *circus*?"

"You've heard the circus is in town. You're desperate to see it. Especially the elephants."

"OK. I'll do it." I get up and do a mock curtsey. "Look, no glasses! Just eyes!"

"I know." He looks up, smiling. "I told you, I love them."

"You love them?" I preen myself.

"You."

Something catches in my throat. His gaze is fixed on mine and there's no doubting what he meant.

"Me too," I manage. "You."

We're sinking into each other's gazes. We're like starving people gorging on cream cakes. But he's challenged me, and I'm not going to wuss out, no way. So I wrench myself away and go to pester a strange blond woman about the circus. I don't look back once, the entire time I'm talking to her. But I can feel his eyes on me all the time. Like sunshine.

Mum's printed us T-shirts. She's actually printed us team T-shirts. We're called The Strategists, which got pulled out of a hat when we couldn't agree on a name.

You wouldn't believe the playroom. It looks like Gaming Central. Ollie and Linus brought their stuff over yesterday, so now there are two desktops (Dad's, which he's lending to me for the match, and Ollie's) and two laptops, each with a chair and a headset and a bottle of water so we stay hydrated. And—last-minute purchase by Mum—a box of Krispy Kremes.

I mean, we could all play online in our own homes. That would be the normal thing. But Mum was like, "OK, if this is a team sport, *play* it like a team sport." And it's a Saturday morning, so actually it works fine.

Mum's suddenly become interested in *LOC*, for the first time in her life, and we've spent all week explaining the characters and the levels and the backstory and answering her dumb questions, like "But why does everyone have to be so *greedy* and *violent*?" In the end, Frank snapped, "It's *Land of Conquerors,* Mum, not *Land of Community Service Volunteers,*" and she did look a bit embarrassed.

I've put in a few hours online and I've sharpened up my game a little. I mean, I'm no Frank. But I won't let them down. I hope. Actually, I think I'm a little better than Ollie, who asked me at our first practice session if I was dating Linus and when I said "Yes," looked deflated for about thirty seconds, then said, manfully, "Well, let's just be good friends and teammates, then." He is quite a cutie, old Ollie.

"I bought some Cokes for the team!" Dad arrives at the door of the playroom.

"Chris!" Mum frowns. "I got them water!"

"One Coke won't hurt."

"Oh God. Look at this." Mum is peering round the room as though for the first time. "*Look* at this room. Coke? Krispy Kremes? Computers?" It's like the triumvirate of all the things she despises and fears. I feel quite sorry for her. "Are we bad parents?" She turns to Dad. "Seriously. Are we bad parents?"

"Maybe." He shrugs. "Probably. What of it?"

"Are we, Audrey?" She wheels round to me.

"Hit-and-miss," I say, deadpan.

"We're not as bad as *these* guys," says Dad in sudden inspiration, and hands her a copy of the *Daily Mail* which he must have bought while he was out. "Read this."

Mum grabs the *Mail* and her eyes fall avidly on a headline.

"*We have to wear identical clothes every day,*" she reads. "*Mum forces her six kids into matching clothes.* Oh my God." She looks up, totally cheered. "We're *so* not as bad as this! Listen, *The children are teased at school, but Christy Gorringe, thirty-two, is unrepentant. 'I like my kids to match,' she says. 'I buy my fabric wholesale.'*" Mum shakes her head in disbelief. "Have you seen them?"

She turns the paper round so we can see a lineup of six miserable kids, all in matching spotted shirts.

"That's made my day!" Mum hastily adjusts her expression. "I mean, poor kids."

"Poor kids." Dad nods.

"But at least we're not as bad as that." She hits the paper. "At least I don't make my children wear vile matching clothes. Things could be worse."

I don't know where Mum would be in life without the *Daily Mail.*

MY SERENE AND LOVING FAMILY—FILM TRANSCRIPT

INTERIOR. 5 ROSEWOOD CLOSE. DAY.

The camera (held by Dad) shows the playroom littered with empty Coke cans and water bottles.

Seen from behind, Frank, OLLIE, Linus, and Audrey are playing *LOC* intensely. Mum is looking from screen to screen, peering over their shoulders and trying to follow, without success.

> **FRANK**
> Go on him. *Jesus.*

He clicks madly and his screen explodes in graphics.

> **MUM**
> (alertly)
> What was that? Which one's you?

> **LINUS**
> Initiate. Initiate.

> **AUDREY**
> Stay in the trees. Nooo! Ollie, you noob.

Ollie is desperately clicking, his face red.

> **OLLIE**
> Sorry.

Mum's head is swiveling wildly from screen to screen.

> **MUM**
> Are you dead? What happens when you die? How can you keep up?

                              FRANK
        Fireblast the fucker. Die! Die!

                               MUM
                            (shocked)
        Frank!

A series of Russian swearing comes from the audio
Skype link.

                              FRANK
          Na kaleni, cyka.

                               MUM
        What does that mean? Is that in the game?

                              LINUS
        It's Russian. You don't want to know
        what it means.

                               MUM
        So is that chap a Russian? Or is that
        you, Frank?

She points at the screen.

                               MUM
        I mean, they all look the same to me.
        Do they look the same to you, Chris?

The camera (held by Dad) focuses in on a screen.

                        DAD (VOICE-OVER)
        Of course they're not the same. Die!
        Die!

We didn't win. Not only did we not win, we were stomped.

Mum was genuinely shocked. I think she'd mentally checked us in for the finals in Toronto and the six-million-dollar prize pot, with her lording it over all the other parents.

"So, how did they beat you?" she said in astonishment when we'd finally got it through to her.

"They played better," said Frank despondently. "They were really good."

"Well, you're really good too," says Mum at once. "You killed loads of people. I mean, you have great technique, Frank. Doesn't he, Chris? Very good technique."

You have to love Mum. She's now behaving as though the only thing she rates in life is *LOC*.

"Anyone want the last Krispy Kreme?" she says, and we all shake our heads. It's a pretty sad atmosphere in here, what with the silent computers and the Coke cans and the air of defeat, and I think Mum realizes this.

"Well, anyway!" she says brightly. "We'll go out for a team lunch to celebrate the taking part. Pizza Express, everyone?"

"Cool." Frank takes off his headset and switches off his laptop. "And then I might go in to the Fox and Hounds," he says casually. "Ade said I could help in the kitchen or whatever at weekends. I need to talk to the head chef. I'll give Ade a ring now, sort it out."

"Oh." Mum looks a bit flummoxed. "Well . . . OK, Frank. Good idea!" As he lopes out of the room, she turns to Dad, her jaw sagging. "Did I hear that right? Is Frank *getting himself a job*?"

But Dad can't hear. He's put on one of the headsets and is logged into another *LOC* game with Ollie.

"Dad, can you play?" I say in surprise.

"Oh, I've picked up a bit," he says, and clicks furiously. "Here and there."

"But who are you playing with?"

"A couple of friends from school," says Ollie, who is equally engrossed. "They were online, so . . . Go on him!"

"I'm on it," says Dad breathlessly. "Oh, shit. Sorry."

Mum is staring at Dad, flabbergasted. "Chris, what are you doing?" She pokes his shoulder. "Chris! I'm talking to you! Did you hear what I said about Frank?"

"Right." Dad pulls off the headset for a moment. "Yes. I heard. Ground him."

I can't help giggling, and even Mum gives a little smile.

"Get back to the game, you big kid," she says. "But we're

going out in half an hour, OK? *Half an hour.* And I don't care if you have to interrupt the game."

"OK," says Dad, sounding just like Frank. "Great. Yeah. Can't wait." He clicks madly, then punches the air as the screen explodes in colour. "Die, you bastard! Die!"

INTERIOR. 5 ROSEWOOD CLOSE. DAY.

The camera wobbles as someone stabilises it on a
high surface. As this person backs away we see it is
AUDREY, in her bedroom. She hesitates, then peers into
the camera.

AUDREY
So, this is me. Audrey. You haven't
met me yet. I'm probably not what you
expected. Like, my hair's probably
darker or lighter or whatever . . .
Anyway. Hello. Nice to meet you.

She pulls up a chair and looks into the camera for a
while, as though sorting out her own thoughts.

AUDREY
I've been thinking a lot about
everything. And I guess Mum was right
about the jagged graphs thing. We're
all on one. Even Frank. Even Mum. Even
Felix. I think what I've realized is,
life is all about climbing up, slipping
down, and picking yourself up again.
And it doesn't matter if you slip down.
As long as you're kind of heading more
or less upwards. That's all you can
hope for. More or less upwards.

There's another silence. Then she looks up with a
sunny smile.

                              AUDREY

               Anyway. I can't stay. I have an
               important engagement with . . .

She reaches down and produces a large, flat case made
of chrome.

                              AUDREY

               This! Mum bought it for me. It's eye
               makeup. Look.

She opens the palette and starts displaying it proudly.

                              AUDREY

               This is mascara, and this is . . .
               primer or whatever . . .

She makes a face as she surveys the tube.

                              AUDREY

               I have *no* idea what to do with that. But
               Mum's going to show me. I mean, it's
               only lunch at Pizza Express, but Linus is
               coming, so it's kind of a date, right?

Another pause.

                              AUDREY

               I think Mum's really pleased I've got my
               eyes back. She said they were the first
               thing she looked at when I was born. My
               eyes. They're me. They're who I am.

Audrey plays around with the lid of the palette for a
few seconds, then closes it and addresses the camera.

                              AUDREY

               Anyway. This has been fun, making
               this film. I mean, not always fun,

but mostly. You know. So. Thanks for
watching, whoever you are.

A pause—then she gives the most dazzling, radiant
smile.

                    AUDREY
          So I guess that's it. I'll turn off
          now.

As she comes close to turn off the camera, Audrey's
blue eyes loom large, filling the screen. She blinks a
couple of times, then winks at the camera.

                    AUDREY
          See you.

ABOUT THE AUTHOR

Sophie Kinsella is a bestselling writer and former financial journalist. She is the author of many number one bestsellers, including the hugely popular Shopaholic series. She has also written seven bestselling novels as Madeleine Wickham. She lives in London with her husband and family.

Visit her online at sophiekinsella.com

Follow Sophie Kinsella on

CATCH UP WITH
BECKY BLOOMWOOD!

FROM THE #1 *NEW YORK TIMES* BESTSELLING AUTHOR SOPHIE KINSELLA

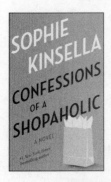

Visit Sophie at www.SophieKinsella.com

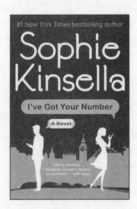